HUNCHING HOMEWARD

A Collection of Short Stories About Lives Disoriented By Vagaries and Vicissitudes in the Human Condition

RICHARD VAUGHN

Cover Graphic By Nan Paturzo

Copyright © 2016 Richard Vaughn
All rights reserved
First Edition

PAGE PUBLISHING, INC.
New York, NY

First originally published by Page Publishing, Inc. 2016

ISBN 978-1-68348-203-1 (pbk)
ISBN 978-1-68348-204-8 (digital)

No part of this book may be used or reproduced by any means, graphic, electronic or mechanical, including photocopying, recording, taping or by any information storage retrieval system without the written permission of the publisher except in the case of brief quotations embodied in critical reviews and articles.

Printed in the United States of America

Also by Richard Vaughn

SOLDIER BOYS
MESA BEACH
CHILDHOOD COUNTRY
RAPTURE RUNNER
PARLOUS PASSION
SOSHAL SCIENTZ

For all the members of my immediate family as well as ancestors and people who haven't managed to show up yet; I am sure they will be along in their own good time.-

"Be fair, or foul, or rain, or shine
The joys I have possess'd, in spite of fate, are mine.
Not Heaven itself upon the past has power,
But what has been, has been, and I have had my hour."
                         -- Horace, 29th Ode

"No one asks to be born. From the second we arrive it's a race against death. Our life involves hunching homeward into the cosmic ocean of existence. Since the end is sure, the purpose of racing lies in doing it as well as possible, not only for our frail selves but also other family who'll follow and owe a bit of essence to us, thereby repaying our debt to the racers who came before."
                         -- Anonymous

CONTENTS

Preface 11

His Mother's Son..13
Chirkey 21
Rural Redemption...26
Beat Of The Drum 35
Filial Suspension 40
An Elderly Man...45
River Child 50
Sawdust Angel 54
Failure In Kind..61
Demolition Man 66
Wading Deep Memory 71
Bad Influence 78
The Warehouse 86
Patchworking 92
Slouch...101
The Guy She Chose 106
Hunching Homeward 116

The Hallelujah Kid	123
Catacombing	129
The Mountain Trail	135
When Gods Walk The Earth	142
Stories Told, Lies Denied	150
Life Models	157
Oldy & Weaking	162
Climbing Mt. Ti'en	170
A Palace Incident	178
Sitting Room Only	184
Toothless Old Man	190
Cleo's Serpent	196
An Old Mirror	201
Weep No More	207
Turn About	213
Respiration	219
About the author	225

PREFACE

Stories seem to simply appear from the human atmosphere. At least that has been my special circumstance in life. With beginning of consciousness around four or five years old, I always made up stories (lies in the world of a child) to deal with a confusing and altogether insane reality. Other creatures were excessively huge, their behaviors incredibly nonsensical, and to make everything completely incomprehensible – they assumed my destiny was to be totally under their control. The only possible defense I could manage was to use my slight powers imaginatively to put them, at least metaphorically, in their place – which I did. Fantasizing everyday in every possible way, they were nominally bent to my childish will.

Of course, getting along in years required considerable modification of this technique, and like most enslaved human beings, I was forced to accommodate socialization and, as they say, work to get along as I, without intent, grew larger and became one of 'them'. It was only after college encounters that I broke loose once again and began consigning people and events to a world of my choosing and of a more satisfying nature. Rejection, failure, disappointment, faults exposed and suffering could be ameliorated through fiction; and even victories, happiness and occasional accomplishment relived for endless enjoyment retrospectively. Stories became my addictive fix without the criminal onus of government controlled substances.

Regardless of my station in life, career ups and downs, personal relationships on line or woefully off the rails, there was always a story excursion available to soothe, comfort and satiate, as well as hurl vengeance, hatred and calamity upon real world malefactors and ill fortune in general. It was, in short, a heaven-sent ability. Although it required effort through isolation, quiet time, and the inevitable reputation for being antisocial, remote, standoffish and 'peculiar', it was worth all shunning to be alone with the literary demon. For, despite the benefits, it at times became a devil with demands sometimes beyond my reckoning. Daydreaming during important practical issues, misreading people who deserved better of me, and otherwise behaving badly and hurtfully. That was a costly burden often regretted. Nonetheless, stories pored forth, and readers, such as you in front of these words, have apparently made an initial choice to confront them.

My best to you, quite literally, in the following pages. I sincerely wish you well as you invest yourself in me. Perhaps as you experience a bit of how I've tried to make life more tolerable, remedies will emerge that will be of assistance to you. I hope so. We all need coping styles as well as actual friends to muddle through this remarkable experiment of awareness in a cosmos that, at least objectively, doesn't reveal much concern for us. But, we'll see about that; science marches ever onward. Thank you for considering my subjective forays into temporary sanity.

Mission Viejo, California (June 2016)

HIS MOTHER'S SON

W ho can remember the day they were born? Nobody. But Robert imagined it as a heavy moist fog, like being smothered in a wet gray blanket until it was thrown off and he emerged from an opaque nothingness into turmoil. Many years later when his mother lay dying in a convalescent home, a grayish room with hospital-like linoleum luminous in the fluorescent light and an ever-present aroma that, despite his knowing that it was disinfectant, the sopping blanket nightmares of his childhood came back. Most children seem to dream of falling only to awake in tumbling terror in the dark of night. He felt pressed under a blanket so laden with brackish water that it seemed saturated with runny cement. His dreams and terrors carried an alien stigma as if from someone else's life.

His first recollection must have been when he was five, perhaps six. She sold cosmetics door-to-door in those days after divorcing his father. She would traipse in bundled against the North Dakota winter in a threadbare wool coat, her auburn hair and face covered with a scarf that left only her pale blue eyes peering out at the frigid world. By the time she removed her galoshes steam would be rising from moist fabric like human smoke. He felt secretly comforted that she worked so hard for his wellbeing and fearful that she might fail and plunge him into catastrophe. Several years later, perhaps 1939, a man and woman visited, and his mother said the man was his father with a second wife. That made no sense, but the man gave him two quarters, bounced him energetically on his knees, and also handed his mother bits of paper money before leaving, cigar smell lingering in Robert's flannel shirt that lasted until another washing.

The next memories that seemed carved into his brainpan with a knife were the bad times with *her* second husband, the bulky man who was put into the VA mental hospital due to World War I disability. What stuck in Robert's mind was the interrogation in a large office with wood paneling and leather chairs. He pictured his mother, and Dr. Dredland, a kindly man with flabby pale skin and reddish hair, and two other men who were deep-voiced and frightened him with stern glances. He listened to them without having to remember because nobody seemed terribly interested in him, unlike when called upon in school to recite gibberish. He was surprised when the thin serious man spoke his name, revealed a yellow-teeth smile, and said he needed to ask Robert a few questions.

Did he, Robert, know what this meeting was about? He shrugged, nervous, sensing the dreadful folds of a blanket closing around him. The man explained that they were interested in determining the fitness of Mr. Harold Brogan, his mother's husband, to remain at home rather than go to the hospital. Did he understand that? He nodded, which was a lie, since Mr. Brogan had already left from home into the hospital, so what more could they talk about? Did Robert know what it meant to tell the truth? Once again he nodded, wondering what he'd done wrong that they had to ask him such a thing. Would he try really hard to answer true, they asked, and not lie about anything? He nodded with a look at his mother because the wet blanket itched his flesh, but she only smiled in her pinched-lip way.

The sober-faced man wanted to know if Mr. Brogan yelled and was angry in the house very often? Robert said yes, but his new father was gone most of the time on the job with the railroad. Of course, but when he came home, how did he behave? Robert did not reply, waiting for help. Did Mr. Brogan sometimes raise his voice to Robert's mother? Yes. Did he grab her or in any way try to hurt her? The blanket, damp and clammy, descended around him from above like an oppressive drapery, covering his head and dripping warm moisture onto his face, hot, salty water that ran down his cheeks and brought stinging sniffles. He nodded and wiped at his eyes with both fists. How often did Mr. Brogan do such things? Lots of times, Robert said. Did Mr. Brogan ever strike or punch his mother? Uh huh. She sobbed in whispers, grasped a tissue, and wiped her eyes before blowing her nose with squeaky, bird-like sounds. The man puckered his lips as if sucking a gumdrop and gazed at his partner and Dr. Dredland.

For a few minutes the men talked to each other in quiet voices, Dr. Dredland explaining some things while Robert and his mother waited. His face had dried by then, but he had trouble breathing and gulped air in deep spasms. The second of the serious men clasped his hands and leaned across the desk closer to Robert. His voice came croaky like a frog's; his tone sounded more serious than the other man. Did Robert remember the night when Mr. Brogan yelled and got really angry? Robert nodded, breathing deep with the memory. When was that? He didn't know for sure. Well then, could he simply tell what happened? Robert felt so weighed down under the heavy blanket that he swallowed hard and held his breath as he remembered the shouting that had awakened him that awful night and made him scurry toward the lighted kitchen, bare feet chilled on the hardwood floor as his skin goose pimpled.

What did you see? the man asked him. Mr. Brogan, in pants and undershirt, waving his arms, yelling, slapping his mother, and waving something in her face as she tried to pull away. The room got terribly quiet as the two men, Dr. Dredland and his mother, stared at him. What did you do? Nothing. Nothing? He said he was too scared to do anything. Why was he afraid? He didn't know. Was Mr. Brogan holding anything in his hand? Uh huh. What was it? A gun. You mean the revolver he used on his job? Uh huh. What was he doing with it? He was waving it around. That's all? He was pointing it at his mother while she cried and said not to. What did Robert do then? He told them he started to cry. What happened after that? His mother got him a glass of water and put him back to bed.

Three years later, he and his mother were in California. The war was raging and she had married yet again, a high school sweetheart who was deferred from the military because he had an essential war job in the oil fields. But he drank a lot, and they fought, and his mother cried while Mr. Kalmer yelled. When Robert acted bad he got whipped with a thick leather belt, sometimes so hard that he couldn't sit for a few days and had to sleep on his stomach. Those beatings stopped after Robert went to junior high school, but Mr. Kalmer still yelled at him and hit him when drinking whiskey. He stayed away from the house as much as he could.

Robert left home at seventeen to join the army and came back two years later after Mr. Kalmer had been killed in an automobile crash. His mother was once again on her own. When she took up with Burt Skedwell, Robert left home again to live near the Junior College. After she divorced Mr. Skedwell, Robert was summoned as a witness when the man sued his mother to get paid for work he had done around her house. Robert didn't know what repairs the man had made but did his best to be truthful, admitting that the back bedroom addition wasn't there the year before. His mother had to pay Mr. Skedwell money she thought he didn't deserve.

Later in the 1950s she dated a lawyer who never seemed to have any clients and was usually working on some deal to negotiate the return of stolen travelers cheques or bank bonds with sleazy characters. Robert was at the house when police detectives came to ask his mother questions about Dave Rikard's whereabouts and had he been in contact with her lately? She didn't know much about anything, cried while she smoked, and Robert kept sneezing and coughing because cigarette smoke bothered his sinuses. It was remarkable that one officer, a swarthy man with light blonde hair and pearly black eyes, took to his mother. She was into her forties by then, but still vivacious with a come-hither manner that was totally unconscious and made her look years younger. They dated for a few months, but nothing came of it to Robert's momentary relief because she later married Deeter 'Doc' Marshall, the used car salesman she had met while buying a pre-owned blue Cadillac convertible.

By then Robert had become completely disgusted with her carrying on and realized that his mother was engaged in a childish struggle to attain the good life which had eluded her since she had left high school. He discovered from his grandmother, that his mother had been royally spoiled by her father. Clothes and jewelry enabling her to party with the Minneapolis debutantes who had money to burn. But when she got out on her own during the 1930s with tough times in the country, there was no way she could even approach a decent living, let alone grandeur. Thus, she was constantly on the lookout for someone who could provide financial security, if not real luxury. It was, Robert told her during their frustrating, argumentative encounters, an unrealistic dream. She persisted in that pursuit of wealth, gambled on horses and lotteries, and got advice from fortunetellers.

Fate and the gods were against her. 'Doc' died in an auto accident on his drive back from a dealer convention in San Diego, an unfortunate collision with a moving van on a fog-shrouded highway. Most of what little estate he possessed had to go to the first wife and children. After, Mother worked at a variety of selling and clerical jobs until she met Russell Seward, a leather-faced retired carpenter. They married and bought a small, wood-frame white house in Glendale. But he also was a heavy drinker, which she disliked and claimed she hadn't known about until after the marriage. She put up with it because Russell was quiet and didn't cause her near the trouble she'd had with her other husbands. Robert stayed away.

When she had a fall in a hospital shower stall after another of her numerous operations-- varicose veins, appendectomy, hemorrhoids, hysterectomy--she was persuaded to sue by an ambitious attorney. Since Robert had been visiting her when the slip occurred, he found himself once more being asked questions about her life and circumstances. His testimony was gratuitous and not particularly helpful. She lost the case, owed attorney fees, and declared bankruptcy. By then the marriage to Russell had turned into bored disdain. They separated and divorced. She was once again alone as Robert lived his own life as best he could. She demanded occasional help of a financial or emotional nature, and eventually, after she retired on Social Security, went to stay with her brother in Portland.

That also did not work out. She smoked a lot, ate chocolates, and found she hated to keep house for a widower who had always been taken care of by his wife. What she most wanted, and desperately needed, was someone to take care of her without imposing on her independence and freedom. She moved into a senior apartment complex and fended for herself. It was the one time Robert remembered not worrying about her, but wondered when she would involve him in more of her problems or escapades. When she reached her eighties, things fell apart.

She had trouble managing her checking account and was in constant, futile arguments with the bank. She spent what little savings she had accumulated on fortunetellers, lotteries, costume jewelry, and commemorative plates, and sent checks to every bogus charity that asked for a contribution. When the dank climate finally affected her delicate lungs, it was necessary to arrange for her move to Los Angeles where he could look after her when she needed help. Her stubbornness made that exhausting. Although her health declined and she had surgery for lung cancer and kidney removal, she refused to stop smoking or eat wholesome meals. When she could no longer be alone and was placed in a convalescent home, her mind already a wandering juxtaposition of memories and fantasies, he found visits with her a tedious exercise in false recollections and demented sensibilities.

There were times when she thought Robert was her father, then her grandfather, sometimes her brother, and once in a while, her son. When he realized she would soon be gone leaving great, regrettable gaps in his life history that would never be filled, he asked about his childhood experiences and troubles. She evaded most questions or bewailed the hard times she'd lived through in the Great Depression.

Her happiest times, she said, were when she was in high school and could go to parties with the 'swells' as she called them, and also the first two years of the war when she had a good paying job and could carouse with the girls she worked with who were single or had husbands and boyfriends in the service. Her reminiscences were devoid of regret or remorse, recalling only the few good times that she felt had made her life worth living. Robert never did learn what she thought about everything she had put him through: stepfathers, numerous houses, apartments, two or three schools each year. When she breathed her last in a morphine-induced coma and the male nurse reported that she was 'gone,' Robert patted his mother's silvery-thin hair and eased the soft gray blanket over her sad face. At last he truly sensed what it meant to be born again.

CHIRKEY

What rang in my ears was the laughter of fellow second graders. Mrs. Wildmon, our teacher, told us to stand and describe what we would be eating on Thanksgiving Day. When my turn arrived I said we'd have 'chirkey' stuffed with cornbread dressing. After the outburst of hilarity subsided, Mrs. Wildmon chuckled, "Don't you mean turkey?"

I repeated, "Chirkey."

"No," she corrected me, "the word is *turkey*. You must use the right word."

I began to feel sick to my stomach, but swallowed hard, shook my head, and said in a dry quavering voice that for sure we were going to have stuffed chirkey. She became stern, gray eyes glassy slits, mouth tight as if slashed with a knife. She bade me sit, and then with that grim tone that made the class stop breathing, she said that we'd get back to the topic of Thanksgiving on Monday. We would each report in *writing* what we actually dined upon. She glared at me as the bell released us into our four day Thanksgiving vacation, and kids sniggered as I walked home through bitter cold.

It was 1939, and I knew in my boyhood way that times were bad. Mother and I lived in rented rooms. That's why I attended different schools because we moved for reasons I never understood but made her cry so deep and long the only thing that calmed her was when I sat nearby sniffling in my own pitiful way.

She sold cosmetics door-to-door. That's how she met widow Platte who lived in a house with a spare room. We moved there in October, which put me in a new school again. I told the truth in class when I said we were going to have chirkey because that's what Mrs. Platte told me. I had watched her un-wrap two weird-looking feathered birds which she placed in a scalding pot even before plucking all the pin feathers off them.

Mom was late getting home for supper that night, weary from trudging through wet snow peddling her wares. Mrs. Platte sat her down near the stove and poured hot coffee. The scrawny birds lay pimpled and yellow on the plank counter. Mother said something about the old pullets looking fresh and ready to be stuffed, but Mrs. Platt hushed her with a wrinkle-faced look toward me, stated that it was chirkey. Mom sighed, tousled my hair, and went to wash up for supper. We had cheese macaroni, and bread pieces in milk sprinkled with cinnamon and sugar for dessert. I later on examined the ground up mound of chirkey on the counter-- now unlike any bird I'd ever seen--and wondered if it was all a joke and I was being made a darned fool.

I wanted somebody to tell me the truth, but I couldn't bring myself to ask. Mother drank coffee, smoked cigarettes while she and Mrs. Platte, whom she called Leni, talked about Mrs. Platte's ne'er-do-well cousin coming for Thanksgiving. I didn't sleep much that night, listening to a fierce Dakota gale pelting ice-beads against the storm window. At breakfast the kitchen was rich with an aroma from the oven. I tried to see what it was when Mrs. Platte basted the crusted brown object, but couldn't because she blocked my view with her gingham and apron bulk.

Her cousin Roscoe, a scarecrow gangly guy with white thatches in his black hair that made it seem like he'd been splashed with paint arrived at noon. His tiny nose was beaked and his green eyes almost gold. For a man who was supposed to be worthless, he smiled a lot and related stories about his travels. We lounged on the parlor sofa while Mrs. Platte and Mother fussed in the kitchen. Roscoe talked about Texas, Nebraska and Iowa. It seemed he'd been just about everywhere and acted like a big shot. He wore faded jeans like mine, except baggy, while my let-out pair felt tight; his clodhopper shoes had thin, turned-up soles. He kept brushing his long hair back behind his ears till most of it draped over his wool shirt collar.

I couldn't get my mind off the cooking smells from the kitchen. Roscoe told Mrs. Platte the train had arrived about dawn and he'd taken time to clean himself up at the Salvation Army before coming over, I asked about the trip. He shrugged and said riding the rails wasn't much to talk about, mostly cold, damp, smelly, and darned uncomfortable unless there was straw.

"Is that like *walking the rails* where kids try to go farthest before falling off?" I asked.

He grinned and shook his head. "No, when empty freight cars pass, it's a shame to waste the space, so men climb aboard to take them between towns." Listening from the kitchen, Mrs. Platte laughed out loud. Roscoe turned and said, "Dang sight better than hoofin' it!"

When we finally sat down for our Thanksgiving meal, the table had bowls of mashed potatoes, turnips, carrots, biscuits, blueberries, and a platter just for the chirkey. It looked like a golden meatloaf with two bird legs stuck at each end.

Mrs. Platte said grace, thanking Lord God for our bountiful blessings. I glanced at Roscoe, who stared at the chirkey. He said it looked the *goldangedest* creature he ever saw. Mrs. Platte frowned, looking my way. I blurted that it wasn't exactly what other folks were having on Thanksgiving, and the school kids thought I was dumb when I told we were having chirkey. Mother patted my head and told me I should be grateful.

I didn't mean to cry and make it worse, but my cheeks were wet. I felt awful. Everyone sat quietly for a while. Then Mrs. Platte passed the mashed potatoes, and Mother and Roscoe served up and passed other dishes around. When he got up with the carving knife and slowly began slicing the chirkey, he spoke about a horrible blizzard in Texas one time when he spent time in a shack and had only "jackalope" for food, a critter that tasted like rabbit and antelope. Now *chirkey* was quite a treat because they're scarce on the prairie these days, he said. This was the first he'd seen in years. He praised Mrs. Platte for finding one so tender and tasty. Most folks had to settle for turkey on Thanksgiving, but old-fashioned chirkey--a traditional critter used by the pioneers moving west across the great plains--well folks, what a special feast!

Our plates now filled, I took a few bites, holding off on the leg portion placed before me. Eventually I dug in, ate heartily, and let myself be kidded by Roscoe. For dessert, I got two huge portions of fruit cocktail-laced, grape Jell-O.

Afterward, while the women washed up in the kitchen, I told Roscoe I needed a holiday dinner report for school on Monday. He said that would be exciting because of our *unique* meal, and he gave advice while I wrote slowly and neatly on my lined tablet.

On Monday, I related a history of the chirkey: a wild animal that roamed the American frontier, but was now nearly *extinct*. Most folks had turkeys bought in meat markets, but I had enjoyed a tasty *repast*. Unlike turkeys, chirkeys have four legs--just enough drumsticks for all who dined at our Thanksgiving table. That, and family together, was a blessing.

When I finished my report, Mrs. Wildmon, grinned and thanked me. Not one kid laughed when I sat down. It was a wonderful and memorable Thanksgiving after all.

RURAL REDEMPTION

When I first entered to gather breakfast eggs, the dank feathered foulness of the henhouse revealed rows of nesting layers. There were five eggs in the basket, retrieved despite beak-snaps at my hand, when a groan startled me and I whirled around. Except for that sound, and a rise and fall of his chest, the man lying on scattered straw looked dead. He had matted gray hair and a weathered face, his lanky frame in ragged overalls and a threadbare denim jacket.

My first notion was to get out, but I didn't have enough eggs. I felt about in the nests but had an odd feeling he was watching. I gazed into the largest blue eyes I'd ever seen as sunlight pierced slits in the planks and revealed burnished skin crinkled like dried earth. I backed into the wood rack of nesting hens. He leaned on one elbow.

"Hiya, kid," he said, and coughed before he spat a gob.

He raised himself until sitting, legs stretched straight on the dusty ground. He'd wrapped feedbags around both legs for warmth and fussed kicking them off.

"Who's Coletta to ya?" he said, clearing his throat.

"My aunt, sorta," I blurted, feeling a real fool.

"Ya're Carteret's boy, are ya?" he rasped.

"He's my step-dad, not my father."

"Yeh, so that's the way of it?" He coughed some more and wiped his eyes with a red bandana. "Figured ya to be Carteret's kid."

"No, I'm not. Only visiting Aunt Coletta." He peered at me while I remained unable to move, which caused me to repeat, "Visiting."

"Where ya from--Jamestown?"

"After Pearl Harbor. Till Mom gets set in Fargo."

"Where's Carteret. He around somewhere?"

"He's...I don't know. He and Mom divorced."

"No surprise. Coletta's the best one in that clan."

"So, that's what I'm doing here--gathering eggs."

"Yeh, well, ya better get on with yar chore then."

I collected seven more eggs and left, closing the plank door. It was a short walk to the back porch. Smoke wafted in curly brown wisps from Aunt Coletta's cast iron stove chimney. I trudged carefully to avoid a stumble and broken eggs. That happened my first visit last summer. Now here I was farmed out once again. The weather was mid-March warm. Snow lay like piles of mashed potatoes across the flat fields with black soil humps and stub shocks of winter wheat poking up like buried animals. The cool air smelled of iron-rich soil and lush grain, but the sun created an ice-melt off the steel corncrib roof.

I stomped mud-caked galoshes on the back porch, kicked them off, shucked my corduroy jacket, and went into the kitchen. Aunt Coletta was in her red check dress with an *Oberton Grain Co-op* sack cinched around her waist. She glanced at me, angular and pinched, but not unkindly, as I put the egg basket on the oilcloth-covered table.

"You look mighty strange, Robby," she said.

"A chill wind," I said, cheeks fiery in the kitchen.

"Nothing to fret about," she said as she flipped sizzling bacon strips with a long-handled fork. "We'll get a late blizzard before long. You'll be in Fargo by then."

I thought about the man in the henhouse. There were men wandering the roads seeking work or on the way somewhere else--ragged, haggard, and needing a meal or a place to rest up before moving on. They'd chop wood, weed gardens, pitch hay and then be gone. With the war and crops to be planted as well as harvested, Aunt Coletta had a hard time finding men to work the fields. She prayed help would arrive, but I didn't see how that'd have much effect since the world went its way regardless what folks desired. But I sensed the weird man amid the chickens was more than passing through.

"There's a man in the henhouse," I said as calmly as I could.

"Uh huh." She put fried bacon on the drain board tea towel.

"I'm guessing he must've sacked out there last night."

"Well, it's comfortable enough for that lately."

Her husband, Hiram, died of a heart attack some years back, and Jarrold, her son, an odd man with straw-thatch hair, had run off and joined the Marines after Pearl Harbor. Last summer he hardly said a word. I figure he was just one of those men who had little to say. If he thought about things, it never showed in word or deed.

"The man's scraggly and looks beat down," I said.

She stared, and then nodded. "Sky-looking eyes?"

That was an eerie question. "Yeah, sorta."

"Huh!" She poked bacon. "Wardy's back."

"Who's that?"

"Wardel Quist, Hiram's kin."

"What's he doing here?"

"Used to work the place. Gambled and drank the wages he got hiring out. He and Hiram didn't get on. Lazy creature. Suppose he wants a handout."

"Won't you need help with Jarrold gone?"

"Not Wardy. He's all talk and no tune. How many eggs did you get?"

She eyed the basket, sighed, forked bacon strips from the skillet and slid in a bowl of sliced potatoes. They crackled in the grease. She was oddly quiet. Unlike most women I had known, Aunt Coletta talked a lot. Whether cooking, washing, tending her vegetable garden, or sewing, she talked, mostly God and Glory. Regardless of the troubles we were to endure during our brief sojourn on earth, Eternal Life was what mattered. Her religion took some getting used to. Although I'd been to Sunday schools when Mom and I moved about, she never went with me. I got the idea religion was for teaching kids to behave.

Aunt Coletta swallowed the Old and New Testaments whole and chewed them into an endless sermon. She read the Bible each day, hummed or sang hymns while she puttered, and often I found her sitting quiet with her head bowed and assumed she was praying or napping. When I crept close, her eyes popped open as if I'd interrupted a private session with her and Lord God Almighty. Being saved she took seriously, and me as a ripe soul for salvation.

"Hiya, Coletta," our visitor said, having snuck in while we fixed breakfast.

"Wardy," she said, not looking at him. She waited to take a deep breath and wipe her eyes with her sleeve. "Wash up."

He went to the sink and began slathering his hands with a cake of lye soap and even splashing his face several times. He didn't seem much bigger than me, and I was right-size for nine years. He dried off with the flour sack towel and watched as she cracked eggs and plopped them into the skillet with the fried potatoes. When the frying was finished she dished up. I sat at my place on a wood chair by the table. Wardy sat to her right after she seated herself. She still had not looked at him.

"Thank thee, Lord," she intoned. "Amen."

"Amen," I mumbled, and pitched in as Wardy grinned.

He waited till Aunt Coletta started to eat, and then he picked up his fork, holding it like a child, and ate with deliberate chewing as if contemplating each mouthful. It was so unusual to be at table without her talking that I felt anxious, and the food that always tasted fresh went down like oily sawdust. Finally, she glanced at him.

"Fixing to stay?' she said.

"Not sure, Coletta."

"Been working?"

"Wahpeton."

"Minnesota?"

"Not for long."

"Still farm jobs?"

He shrugged. "Sure."

"War work's starting."

"Yeh, heard about that."

"Jarrold's gone away."

"Figured he might."

"Could use you here."

"Reckoned as much."

I'd only eaten half my breakfast and wondered what was on their minds that they weren't saying. When they fell quiet, it came like silent prayer at church. For a while the only sound was forks tickling our plates, slurping and gulping as they drank black coffee and I drank milk. When they finished eating before I did, they sat up straight, poised stiff as statues, watching me finish. This was the oddest breakfast ever, and in my brief years I'd eaten in diners, hotels and boarding houses. Without his asking, she refilled Wardy's coffee mug and they drank as I ate the last piece of bacon. I didn't know how long we'd stay like that but didn't think it was my place to do much. She wiped her mouth with the corner of her apron and patted Wardy's brown left hand with her pink, veined right hand. It was such a tender gesture she let her hand linger.

"Stay or go as it suits you," she said.
"That I will," he said, relieved, I sensed.
"The Lord will watch over you as always."
"Even if I haven't been saved?" he grinned.
"Specially if you haven't. I pray for Jarrold, too."
"Wasn't Jarrold saved a couple years back?"
"Hook didn't set, but I have hope everlasting."
"If he gets into hard combat, that'll sure do it."
She folded her hands. "You didn't find God."
"Yeh, that's true. Just my stubborn way."
"What war was that?" I blurted.
"France," he said. "In 1918."
"Fighting the Germans?"
"We called them Huns."
"Did you kill anybody?"
"No, kid, only myself."

I stared at Aunt Coletta, who shook her head and said nothing.

"Got gassed," Wardy said, gazing down at his empty plate as he spun the coffee mug with both hands. He appeared quite old, frail, with wrinkles like my grandfather. He couldn't be that old. Yet there he was, slouched at Aunt Coletta's table like a man near the end of his life. Wardy shrugged. "Sometimes, kid, it don't pay to keep breathing."

"Don't say that," she said. "Robby doesn't need rubbish talk."

"Yeh, well," he said, wiping his mouth on his flannel shirtsleeve. "All the same, if this new war don't do us in, it'll be a goddamned miracle."

"If you'd found it in your heart to be saved," she said, "you wouldn't shame this table with such blasphemy. We don't damn God, or anybody else, in this house."

"I was praising the Lord," Wardy said. "It'll take something miraculous to keep from blowing ourselves to hell and gone. Pray the Japs don't drop gas here."

Aunt Coletta stood up, scraping her chair on the linoleum. She took both her plate and mine to the sink and turned on the faucet. I still had milk in my glass and drank as the room filled with heaviness. Wardy leaned in his chair and rocked, staring at me, and then Aunt Coletta. She began washing dishes. He took his plate over, staying by her with both hands in his overalls pockets and bouncing on booted toes like a child.

"If I hadn't joined up," he said, as much to himself as to her, "it might've been me and you instead of Hiram…when I got back, I mean."

"Is that what you think after all this time?" she said, equally quiet.

"Well, yeh. If I hadn't been in the hospital…not fit for much… we could've…"

"No…Wardy. It wouldn't have been that way ever again. Not like before."

She gazed out the window while morning sunlight streamed onto her face. From where I watched, she appeared hunched over the sink as if preparing to pray or read the Bible. It was intriguing, Wardy swaying as if about to dance, Aunt Coletta moving hands, arms and shoulders to the rhythm of washing and rinsing dishes, her head with streaked gray brown hair cinched with a black comb bun. When she didn't say anymore, he went flatfooted and opened his arms as if about to put them around her.

"It's surely the same old me, Coletta," he said humbly.
"No need to tell what I right plainly know," she said.
"I'll stay for long as ya need some farming help."
"It's up to you, like it's always been before."
He said, "Did ya pray I might stop by?"
"Not one mite more than usual."
"Must be why I showed up."
She grinned a bit. "Hush."
"I'll see what's in the barn."
"You'll find something."
"Ya don't mind my staying?"
"As long as you behave."

Wardy patted my shoulder when he passed by just as I finished drinking the milk. I took the glass to Aunt Coletta and watched her finish washing and rinsing the dishes to a drying rack before retrieving the frying pan to scrub. I grabbed the flour sack dishtowel to start drying. Quiet was still required for the next few minutes till I couldn't stand it.

"How long will I be here?" I asked, hoping Mom would settle fast at her new job in Fargo and want me right away. "I'm supposed to be going to school."

"She'll phone when it's time," she said in her patient way.

It came to me that with her husband dead, son gone to the war, and Wardy only a maybe for help on the farm, I was all she had except neighbor ladies who visited. Her brother, Carteret, was also a war casualty, a mental case who'd terrorized my mother and me till the divorce. As much as I longed to be away from this forlorn farm, it didn't seem proper Aunt Coletta should be alone. How much comfort was God at such a time? Except for Mom and me taking care of each other all those times we roomed with strangers and had to share a bed, this was the first time it hit me hard that folks really needed somebody.

"Will Wardy stay to help out?" I said hopefully.

She passed me a smile. "If the Lord wills it."

"He could sure take care of most chores."

"Yes, if he was of a mind to." She rinsed the skillet and placed it on the drying rack. "But, I expect he'll move on when the mood strikes him."

"But he'll come back again, won't he?"

"He surely will…and then leave again."

She bowed her head; it was the saddest I ever saw her. Wardy stayed for the four weeks till Mom sent a post card and Aunt Coletta put me on a bus to Fargo. I got along okay with him as we did chores. Jarrold died on Tarawa the next year. Later on I heard Wardy finally got saved and lived in amity with Aunt Coletta.

BEAT OF THE DRUM

"Let him go!" were the harshest words I heard my great grandfather say. He spoke from a sick bed in Grandmother's farmhouse in Arbordale. I didn't realize he was so ill and wanted to go outside to play rather than suffer a vigil in the dark room that smelled of liniment, pipe tobacco and dry old man. As if to make it a command to his daughter, who was Ida Mae to me, he went on in his cracked voice. "It's no place fer a boy t'spend a summer's day."

"You shush," she told him. "Robby'll be just fine sitting a spell with you."

He sighed into a growl. "Fine, woman, but y'don't know a lick 'bout boys."

"Know all I need to know about a boy who never grew up," she said, fluffing the pillow under his silvered long hair. With deft strokes she brushed his beard and nudged me to sit in the straight back chair by the bed. "Now, Robby, keep him company."

"So, you're what's left'a the clan, eh boy?" He peered at me with rheumy eyes.

"Don't be talking like that," she said to him. "He's Olivia's son, as you know darn well. Been here since mid-May because she's working in a defense plant in Fargo."

"Tribe's runnin' outta menfolks," he said as Ida Mae whisked past in her flower print dress with a whiff of talcum and lilac water, leaving us alone.

Jason Dean Whitley, Jadee to the family, had outlived my grandfather, who died in 1943. Jadee was now ninety three and the town's last surviving member of the Grand Army of the Republic. Born in 1850, he'd gone to war as a drummer with the Minnesota Volunteers in 1864, part of that vast crusade of adolescent farm boys seeking adventure. Ida Mae showed me photos of Jadee in parades during the 1920s and 1930s with the old soldiers. Most looked decrepit in wide-brim hats and brass-button blue jackets bedecked with medals, but Jadee was youthful and spry in his kepi with its black leather visor--the same cap he wore when we marched in the 1941 Memorial Day parade.

In truth, I marched with a Cub Scout troop while he rode in a convertible with the mayor just ahead of the American Legion band that played *Battle Hymn of the Republic*, *Marching Through Georgia*, and *Rally Round The Flag Boys* many times while he waved to the crowd. It was the first time I realized other folks considered him something special. Afterward, he sat in his rocker in the parlor and told about carrying wounded soldiers on stretchers, drumming tat, tat, rata-tat-tat on long marches, and the time he carried the flag during an assault on Confederate lines in the Shenandoah Valley. He spoke with pride of General Sheridan as if he knew him well, and showed me the medal he got when released from service. The red ribbon had turned orange and the bronze crusted with age, but that didn't diminish Jadee's pride in owning it.

HUNCHING HOMEWARD

I became so enthused about his boyhood adventures that I tired him out pestering with questions until Ida Mae hushed me because it was time for Jadee's nap. He winked at me as if to say we'd talk later, and went to sleep in an instant. His hands twitched and jerked while he slept, and I asked Grandmother if that was from all the drumming he'd done in the war. She said Heaven's no, it was so long ago nobody could remember. He was just having a palsy. But when he woke and I brought it up to him, he had me fetch two of Ida Mae's wooden spoons from the kitchen. He grasped them in his gnarled, veined hands as if old friends, and proceeded to tap on the maple table beside his chair. He did so many I couldn't tell one from another, saying in his quaver that each was an Order of March.

Once again Ida Mae interrupted us for supper and I was left wondering about all the experiences Jadee'd had that were locked in his mind. In the days that followed he taught me how to hold drumsticks. They weren't clutched so much as caressed so they could tap the drum in a natural rhythm that followed a man's heartbeat. Jadee insisted that drumming was nothing but unleashing the pulse of life through arms and hands. It resonated from wood hitting dried skin and encouraged the God-ordained urge to march in unison. That's how men went to war, shoulder to shoulder, facing wounds and death. One time he showed me a minie ball that he unwrapped from a handkerchief. It was copper-colored, patina-aged. It had smacked his drum during an attack, nearly spent as it penetrated the wood and rattled inside while he marched and drummed. It was, he said, the scariest time of his youth, an attack with his fellow drummer boys marching behind an assault line of infantry. Cannon fire roared overhead to blast trenches atop a gradual rise. Rebel shells crashed ahead with fire and smoke, and then into the blue coats amid screams and shouts.

Every explosion rocked the earth under his feet as he gasped and concentrated on the beat--rata-tat-tat, rata-tat-tat--so much thunder in his ears the only way he knew he was still drumming was the slap of the drum against his legs as he marched and snap of the drum sticks. The most peculiar thing, Jadee mused, was that in spite of the awful bedlam, he sensed the balls whizzing past, felt the skin-singeing heat of exploding shells, and heard boys hit around him. It sounded like hail stones during a mid-summer thunderstorm smacking a fresh-plowed meadow, but stank of black powder smoke that made the boys come and go like ghosts.

A man beside him, built solid like a field hand, got hit in the shoulder by a minie ball. It spun him around like a top before he somersaulted backwards and lay groaning. If I wanted to know what it sounded and felt like, he said, I should get me a baseball bat or wagon tongue, and whack the side of a heifer just as hard as I could, and it still wouldn't be close enough to the real thing. When it was time for Jadee to go to bed, Ida Mae took his arm and guided him into his room. Despite his long years, and something she called 'ritis', he stood straight and walked, albeit with a wobble, like a soldier marching--legs forward, back rigid, shoulders square. Life just didn't seem to bow him down no matter how rough it had been.

Before the summer of 1943 ended, he spent more time in bed, still talking to me and telling stories, some of which were the same as before but changed a bit so that I got confused. Sometimes he called for a guy named Toby, then somebody called Josh. They had been boy soldiers with him. Once in a while, after waking, he mixed me up with one of them as he rambled. It got to a point where he was in his room all day. Ida Mae kept me out because Jadee needed rest. That was when, one lazy afternoon, he spoke his last words in my presence. They had to do with his wanting to run away and join the army, his mother's refusal, and his father telling her to let him go, it'd do the boy good. The town doctor came each day to see Jadee and console Ida Mae, who missed Grandpa. She was distraught as she kept rousing the last man in the family when he began to slide into death. The doctor urged her to leave him to God. It was time for Jadee to depart this life.

Later one night I was awakened by sobbing. She sat in the kitchen in her robe and clasped her hands beseeching the Lord to amend the ways of the world. I asked what was wrong. She said she couldn't abide the thought of being left alone after Jadee was taken. I wasn't old enough to grasp most things that came my way. When we heard Jadee choking and struggling for breath in his room, she rose to go and stir him so he couldn't slip away. I hurried behind and saw him in the bed. He lay small as a child, wizened, fingers tapping a cadence on the coverlet. Ida Mae was about to shake him. I eased her back and urged her quietly, tearfully: *Let him go.*

FILIAL SUSPENSION

M y mother wasn't religious but courted the spirit world with such fervor that she would have put a holy man to utter shame. I think she knew God was somewhere and He moved in mysterious and bizarre ways. The most vivid example happened in 1943 when I was ten and we lived in Mrs. Lentzer's basement flat in Fargo. I slept on a day bed in the living room. Late one night I heard Mother talking in her room.

"I don't know what you mean!" she was saying like a perturbed child.

"Are you alright?" I called out. "You going back to sleep?"

"Ohhh, I don't know what to do!" she wailed. "What to dooo!"

I got up, goose bumps like a skinned chicken, and padded across the cement floor to the burlap fabric that served as a privacy curtain into her room. She was half-sitting in bed, her hair in rubber curlers to make her perm last longer. Her blue eyes looked gray in the half-light that spilled through the basement window. She mumbled as if talking to some person unseen. I sat on the edge of the bed. She didn't look at me until a couple minutes passed. When she did, it took a bit before she recognized me and put both hands on my shoulders as she tried to catch her breath.

"Oh, honey," she gasped. "It was so frightful. Pops was here in the room."

That was her father, apparently given to surprise nocturnal visits.

"What did he want this time?"

She often told me that he talked to her at night even though he was in a hospital near Seattle where her brother, Floyd, serving in the navy, could see to him. She didn't answer, looking off into the shadowed twilight of her room as if seeking something she had misplaced. Unlike my sleep area that smelled of the remnants of several meals--meatloaf when we saved enough red ration points for ground beef, potatoes, and onions---her room was scented with creams, lotions, pomades, shampoo, and cologne.

"Pops nudged me in the back," she whispered. "It never ever happened before."

Unlike me, she seemed to dream incessantly. "What did he want?"

"Oh, honey!" She got a cigarette from the Chesterfield pack on the night table, tamped down the tobacco, lit it with a box match and inhaled deeply as if taking in life itself before expelling a desperate puff. "He told me something awful. That I was going to the dogs. That's what he said, to the dogs."

Smoke drifted around her head before spiraling toward the exposed ceiling beams, the underside of Mrs. Lentzer's living room floor. She looked so forlorn that there wasn't much I could say to cheer her up. She worked hard at any job she was able to get, always wanting the best for us in wartime Fargo. I was happy, and didn't mind when she tried to relax with the girls from work. She sometimes had too many cocktails, but wasn't a drunk--mostly mellow, like a young girl at her first party. She apologized the next morning as if she'd behaved horribly. It didn't bother me, and I told her so unless I was down and had a need to spread misery. I didn't feel that way now, slumped on the bed.

"It's okay, Mom. Pops has talked to you like that before, hasn't he?"

"Sure, but not with such force. Not so angry and full of...vexation."

She finished the cigarette, smoked another. My feet had passed feeling cold and turned frigid. She walked me to my bed, tucked me in, and went back to sleep. The next morning during breakfast the phone call came. Pops had died during the night, almost at the time she'd awakened with the dream. She wept before leaving for work as I went off to school. She believed that, at the instant her father died, he came to bestow a message before going into the ghostly world that existed beyond our mortal grasp.

The incident was like her nightmare that Floyd had died somewhere in the South Pacific. That didn't happen, but it coincided with one of his two crash landings in a C-47 he described to me years later. As I said, she didn't care for religion, at least for herself, but sent me to Sunday school at any nearby church. She didn't go, I think, because she didn't want to clutter her soul with anything that might mess up her connection to the awesome realm of the spirit world.

She had a vivid fantasy life, while I never had dreams or nightmares. Aside from the episode with her father that night, she often told me about dreams where she was on an incredible adventure traveling in Europe or Asia, seeing amazing things and meeting strange people. I envied her imagination; she'd never traveled anywhere as far as I knew, so the ability to go places in her mind was a wonderful gift.

HUNCHING HOMEWARD

Often in bed before sleep, I tried to prime my brain for a journey, but nothing happened. I decided that I wasn't cut out for the unique fantasies that graced Mother's everyday life. It produced my disbelief in everything illogical or unscientific; spiritual and mental events were natural aspects of the physical brain and nervous system.

When my grandmother passed away in the same hospital where Mother worked, I assumed that the immediacy and proximity of her death would prevent any transmissions through the ether. I was wrong. Mother told me months later that she had received several messages in her sleep and Grandma was with Pops on the 'other side.' By this time in my young adult life, I paid little attention to such foolishness, only becoming involved when she tried to persuade me that her episodes were as real as life itself. In later years I spent little time with her, keeping in touch through phone calls. Although I avoided inquiring about her unique contacts with the spirit world, she described frequent encounters with Gypsy fortunetellers, tea leaf readers, and Tarot card advisers.

"Mom, I don't believe that silliness, so don't throw it at me.."

"Oh, I know, honey. But just wait a while. You'll see."

"Yeah, I'm sure I will, but not right now."

"Important things happen we can't see clearly."

"Sure, I know, through a glass darkly. I get it."

"Don't be a smart aleck. You'll see when the time comes."

Then she died, in a convalescent hospital. While there I kept expecting signals on her spiritual wavelength, a psychic telegram. Her mind wandered when I visited; she saw me as either Pops or Floyd, and just as often as myself. There was no talk of spirit visits from her mother or father, and she said she didn't dream anymore. Her spiritual life was based upon personal eccentricities aligned with her impressionable childhood. She passed away with a benign smile as if listening to a pleasing song or a welcoming message beamed to her from a place she believed existed and was awaiting her arrival.

Three weeks after her memorial service I was still waiting for a sign that her faith about a realm of pure essence had been validated. It was irrational and sentimental, but I couldn't dismiss eighty years of possibility. Months later after returning to ordinary life, I was aroused in the night by a persistent pressure on my shoulders. My wife slept. I had no aches or pains to account for the eerie sensation. I floated back to sleep on a wave of warm, tropical current in sublime drowsiness, Mother's whispery voice, hummingbird wings feathering my face so delicately my skin tingled with pleasure.

"*Oh, honey! Remember, all things come in their own sweet time.*"

I didn't want to acknowledge her presence. It would denigrate what I'd come to believe. There was no spirit world; it was fantasization. Yet, I became sweat-cold with anxiety; at last, a dream life of my own, exceeding Mother's incandescent foolishness. Like it or not, I was part of the family legacy I'd so long disparaged. Mother had visited on her schedule, not mine. Years later, after my wife died, I confessed to my daughter: *Please don't think me odd, but sometimes your grandmother and mother talk to me. I can't explain how or why, but they do.* My daughter smiled as I said: *Just you wait.* As expected, she nodded and went about her business.

AN ELDERLY MAN

My grandfather died in 1943 when I was ten years old. I mistakenly referred to him as Grandpa Eldon because I'd heard him addressed as 'Eld' when I lived with him and Grandma Ida. When I first became aware of him he was a large, white-haired man with a barrel chest, bushy eyebrows, and folds of leathery facial skin that made his merry blue eyes shine like agates. Ida told me that I asked her one time in Eld's presence if he was an old man because he looked like her father. They laughed as she told me that, no, he wasn't an old man, he was an 'elderly' man. I heard it as an 'eld' man.

I thought about it during the funeral when my mother visited from her wartime job in Minneapolis. I had spent time with Eld and Ida on their farm outside Arbordale. Eld was gone a lot as a farm equipment salesman in Minnesota and the Dakotas. When times went bad and he had a stroke, he retired to the farm that had been worked by hired help. On cold winter days and long nights in the farmhouse, we played games.

RICHARD VAUGHN

I was a railroad engineer and set up train stations in the kitchen through the dining room, parlor and living room, and ran from one to the other. Eld moved about pretending to be a station clerk or passenger getting off the train--my wood wagon. I made engine noises and announced arrivals and departures. Not knowing his precarious health, I was careless about his energy and had to be kept from tiring him by Ida. She shushed me or made me sit in the kitchen while she fixed supper, or oftentimes put me to work kneading biscuit dough or some other chore that allowed Eld to rest.

On cold winter mornings when I had to catch the school bus at the bottom of the hill, Eld helped me into my snowsuit and galoshes on the porch and saw me out the storm door, watching in his wool pants and fuzzy sweater till I was safely seated inside the bus. My black metal lunch box held a sandwich, fruit, cookies and a Thermos of hot cocoa. It anchored me as much to Eld as to Ida, who made sure I had warm clothes and tucked me into bed each night. In later years, dwelling on my childhood, isolated from my mother, I was nonetheless well cared for and even adored at a time when it mattered a lot. They treasured me with a great heartedness that belied their own difficulties.

They'd had hard times. Eld was born in 1863 on the farm that I shared with them till his condition required moving into Arbordale to be near a doctor and town amenities. Like so many farm families in the waning years of the nineteenth century, Eld had to wait until his father died before he could inherit the farm and take on the responsibilities of a wife. He courted Ida for ten years, and when they married in 1903, he was almost forty, late for parenting and, in retrospect, even later for grand parenting.

Ida was born in 1875, a strapping, stalwart farm girl with five sisters and able to have children at the age of twenty-eight when she married. Their son came in 1905, and my mother, Olivia, in 1908. To support his family, Eld had the farm worked by tenants and hit the road peddling farm equipment. He did well enough to rent a fine house in Minneapolis, where they lived until Eld's stroke in 1938. Then they went back to the farm. My mother, divorced from my dad, asked them to care for me as she got her life back to normalcy. That was the term Ida used to describe the situation.

My memory of childhood is those five years from 1938 to 1943 till Eld's death. After, I joined my mother, who'd moved to Fargo, and Ida went to Spokane to live with uncle's family. I was raised by two strong farm people, and mental pictures of growing up are laced with their images, Eld more opaque than Ida since she lived until 1970. I catch glimpses of Eld and me lighting Christmas tree candles, each in a metal cup on a branch with tin pails of water nearby in case flame should touch pine and flare into fire. The glow of those lights has remained forever linked with imminent danger.

He was seated in a huge brocade chair near the fireplace, smoking his cigar and watching Ida set the dining table for supper. I sprawled on the rug with my electric train set. Eld called me over after puffing billows of smoke toward the ceiling. *Would I fancy seeing something magical?* He placed both my hands on his knees while he took a huge pull on the cigar. While I watched, smoke poured forth in a blue-white puff and roiled into a circle around my head. Again! I cried. After the second puff, I felt a hot sensation on my left hand. He held the cigar so close it singed me. I jerked my hand back with a yowl. He chuckled as I squealed. *Got to be careful of tricks.*

While I rubbed the skin, wondering if it hurt bad enough to cry, he asked if I'd like to see another amazing trick. I shook my head. *Even more exciting than the smoke ring? Watch my ears.* He could make cigar smoke come out of his ears. That sounded fantastic. I put both hands on his knees again and he took a big puff while I waited for the smoke to come from his ears. It didn't of course; the cigar warmed my right hand again. I leaped with a squawk as Ida came into the room. Eld tousled my hair while she muttered about nasty stunts and no way to treat a boy. Eld stuck the cigar in his mouth, clasped both my hands, and advised me to be cautious and take life as it comes as Ida grumbled 'Heaven sakes alive' and 'Darned foolishness.'

Eld drove Lincoln sedans when he was in the money, a new car every year. But after the good times, he got a used dark blue Model A Ford. On one trip to town, a gray mouse crept from the air vent below the windshield. It crept from side to side. Eld joked about the new passenger we had awakened starting the car. Although we looked for it when the car was stowed in the barn, we only saw it as it walked around in the fresh air ruffling its fur. On summer Saturday nights I sat on the hood while the car was parked by the Arbordale bandstand. We listened to the American Legion band, a glorious sound to my boyish ears.

I have memories of Eld sitting quietly reading the paper or staring out the front window at winter snow, at spring buds or rain bullets hitting the soil, or quiet summer nights on the porch as he gazed at the stars and moon. He got sick more often in later years, throwing up in a basin by the kitchen, or lumbering up the stairs. The final few weeks he was bedridden and shriveled in the big feather bed. Mother came more often and was there during his last night. One breakfast when I joined Ida and my mother, they told me Eld had passed away in his sleep.

He had no parting words, no worldly wisdom for my boyish ears or direction for my manhood. I figure it was mostly the example of his character--durable, devoted, sober to the point of bursting out with sly trickery or merriment as if some force inside had to be released in tomfoolery. Maybe because he'd had no real childhood of his own, slaving on his stern father's farm till he was able to have a life of his own, he found it enjoyable having me around. I saw him the night he died. Ida and my mother talked with the doctor downstairs while I stood at the foot of Eld's bed. I must've said something about him having a good night. He smiled and waved in such an easy way that it was impossible to believe that he wouldn't still be there in the morning.

    The funeral was well attended considering wartime and gas rationing. Farmers who'd known him in his equipment sales days came up from Mankato and down from Duluth. It was impressive, more than forty people. Ida and Mother stood beside the Lutheran minister. That's when I heard Eld's actual name: Lemuel Francis Kuhneman. He lived eighty years, half in the nineteenth and twentieth centuries--an elderly man who left his beloved Ida behind to love me well into her nineties--till I became a bit more like him, older but not yet elderly.

RIVER CHILD

The flood came to Fargo, North Dakota in Spring '43. I was in the fifth grade, a slight ten-year-old boy. When the principal came into the room and asked if anybody could help at the river, my hand shot up. I was not large, or strong, but would've done anything to skip class. People were needed to fill sand bags, and each boy who helped would get a fifty-cent savings stamp. It was a grown up way to contribute to the war effort. I'd gone last spring to plant onions and swept streets of glass to save tires.

It was only nine in the morning, but a dozen from the fifth grade class joined more boys from sixth grade, piled into a school bus and, after stops at three other schools, drove out of the city. After an hour, the bus stopped at a crossroads by a cluster of tin mailboxes hutched on a wooden rail. Seven farmers and as many hard boys climbed aboard. The boys were scruffy in overalls, corduroy caps with earflaps, and patched jackets; the bus began to smell like manure, mud, and alfalfa. One gray-haired man had a missing right arm, the jacket sleeve hitched half way with a brass safety pin.

HUNCHING HOMEWARD

Nobody said much as the bus groaned along, finally leaving the highway for a muck-packed road along an oak tree line by the river. It jerked to a stop and we got out. My galoshes sank into ooze making it hard to lift each foot. We trudged to the trees, and came upon scrub spruce by the riverbank. A soldier tossed shovels and burlap bags from a flat bed truck. I got a shovel, but the one-armed man took it from me, telling me to carry empty bags.

I stumbled down into an area to be reinforced before the river would surge over a knee-high sand bag wall and saw the brackish-brown water--a tributary of the Red River rampaging toward Fargo. The surface roiled like a monster with its topside bared to the gray sky. Us small boys held bags open as men and big boys shoveled sand from piles dumped by growling trucks. Lunch brought thick-sliced bread and bologna slathered in mustard or mayonnaise. I'd tasted coffee, but this was the first time I'd been given my own mug. It was bitter and hot; I gulped, chewed, and then back to gripping bags as they were filled with sour sand.

I was wearing knit gloves, but my fingers and wrists still got whacked with the edge of the shovel as the one-arm man worked beside me. The wool became so soggy and grimy that I had trouble holding the bag till it was full enough for a man to tie it off with twine, and haul it to the levee. A man shouted about something in the river. We'd already seen haystacks, outhouses and bloated cows with stiff legs. But this looked like part of a tool shed or corn crib roof--with a body stretched across it.

My first notion was Huck and Jim rafting down the Mississippi in *Huckleberry Finn*. There was yelling about the body being a kid, clinging to the timbers as river splashed over it. One large man flung his shovel aside and scrambled along the shore. I slogged behind as if we were partners in a desperate venture. He called out to the child, who raised its head. I saw long, scraggly red hair and a white face. It was a girl! I didn't know how old, but pictured Eliza from *Uncle Tom's Cabin* fleeing across an ice flow.

The large man had a coil of rope that he unwound as if getting ready to lasso a heifer. He flung it as far as he could. The rope splashed into the water short of the roof. The girl lifted up, eyes wide in fright, her lips moving soundlessly. After the rope was hauled in and rewound, the man threw it again. This time it slapped across the back of the girl's jeans. She grabbed hold. After a few shouts, she understood she should tie it about herself under both arms. She did, the hemp cutting taut into her red shirt. She looked like the young sister of some of the farm boys. During this time the man and me had been loping along the riverbank, sliding in mud as we stayed even with the girl. The man pulled the rope, yanked with both hands. Without thinking, I pulled as hard as I could because the girl must weigh a ton or the roof was heavier than it looked. Two farm boys joined us. The man told her to jump off. She hesitated, trembling, but then let go and slipped into the current. That helped us a bit, but pulling was still tough. As the river carried her downstream, we stopped scrambling along the bank to anchor ourselves. The straining rope caused her to drift shoreward.

However, instead of remaining afloat, our pulling seemed to drag her under. That made the large man curse at us to pull faster. We tried, all tugging like maniacs, catching the rope on shrubs and saplings as we strained. Part of a dead tree drifted against the girl. I hoped that might help, give her something to hang on to. But it rolled on top and almost jerked the rope from our hands. The man grunted, dug in his muddy boots, wrapped the end of the rope around his waist, and hung on. The girl had disappeared. That's when despair clutched me--we'd never save her no matter what. Finally, we dragged her in. I helped swag her up onto the grassy slope.

HUNCHING HOMEWARD

The man pumped her chest with his large hands. I was soaked, sick--my gut squishy as I saw water gush from the girl's mouth like pale blood. Her matted hair looked like prairie weeds. She was so childlike, face flour-paste white, eyes blue-gray and cold in death, staring nowhere. She was the first dead person I'd ever seen. Time slowed till the sun squashed on the horizon. Men carried the girl in an army blanket to the bus. Coffee gorge soured me. Nobody spoke during the ride back. At the crossroads by the mailboxes she was put in the bed of a red pickup truck. I got off at the school and collected a savings stamp for helping stem the flood. I glued it into my savings book, sealing more than just a day of my life helping the war effort.

SAWDUST ANGEL

It wasn't the first time I fell in love, but in the least likely place--a revival tent. On an August 1943 Friday night the Prairie Disciplers camped in a grassy field behind Oberton Hardware Store. Lush Dakota plains swept off to the horizon with summer sorghum, corn, and barley ripening for the war effort. Aunt Coletta clutched my hand as we entered the stifling tent. I studied a poster with an angelic girl descending heavenly stairs, pink-robed, blonde ringlets: Thessalie Havenhurst. We jostled onto wood benches amid two hundred farm souls.

This was the second summer I'd spent with Aunt Coletta while Mother worked in Fargo. Aunt Coletta didn't believe in canned food, so I had meals loaded with hominy, spinach, string beans, chicken chunks in cream gravy with dumplings, and helpings of peaches, rhubarb or green apples. What she did believe in was Salvation and praying in the Oberton Gospel Church, along with bouts of religious renewal when a revival came. It was her duty to remind the Lord that her late husband, Hiram, not the godly man he should've been, needed blessing. She also beseeched Him to look after her son, Jarrold, who'd joined the Marine Corps the day after Pearl Harbor.

I'd been to revivals and wasn't surprised this one began with a plump lady in a long blue dress raising her arms and saying it was time to praise the Lord. Behind her, a bald accordionist, gawky trombonist, a boy with a bass drum, and a wizened old man cradling a fiddle thumped *Onward Christian Soldiers,* followed, when we were sweaty and clapping, by *The Old Rugged Cross.* The lady was joined by a stern man with long hair the color of red wheat. His voice, as he told us to pray, was oddly high-pitched.

Then we got the sermon. The preacher's voice turned hoarse, his eyes bulged. He slapped the Bible against his chest, which made dust puff from the black cloth like smoke. The rapt folks yelled 'Amen, Brother,' 'Hallelujah.' and most often, 'Oh Lord God Almighty!' It lasted forever while I searched the stage for the angel shown on the poster. The listless boy with the bass drum resembled her somewhat.

I was shaken from torpor by the band and crowd charging into *When The Roll Is Called Up Yonder.* We were standing, clapping, and I was smothered by gruff farmers and their wives' high voices. When in town, these same people with thin lips and crinkled eyes looked somber, but now they were joyful. That must be what Aunt Coletta meant by *transfigured*, a word she used for people reborn in the Lord. Being transfigured was both possible and a good thing for imperfect mortal humans.

The hymn concluded with rousing 'Amens' and 'Hosannas!' The preacher raised his arms and prayed long and hard for the bounty of the Lord to come forth in an offering from God's own people. Wire-strung lights overhead dimmed and then a spotlight lit the curtain behind a wood ramp. Violin music penetrated my being. The curtain parted, and before us was the angel, a girl in pink robe cradling cornflowers with her left arm while pressing a Bible to her bosom with the other. As if floating down from heaven itself, she descended. There was a hush, the violin like the song of a bird from the Garden of Eden till, faintly, a sweet voice was singing. She sang so softly it was hard to detect the words till she reached the platform. *Jesus loves me, this I know, for the Bible tells me so, He is strong and I am weak.* An old lady behind muttered 'My Dear Sweet Jesus,' while Aunt Coletta clasped my hand as she fumbled for a kerchief.

The girl walked up the aisle behind the ladies and men handling wood milk pails filling up with paper money. When it came along our bench, Aunt Coletta put in a dollar bill, nudged me, and my quarter went into the bucket. I didn't want to part with it, but a look from the angel so undid me that my fingers opened and my pittance of wealth went to the Lord. Her eyes, milk white with blue corneas, pierced my heart. I couldn't breathe and turned to watch her, hair like satin as she floated into the spotlight.

After the ushers returned with the offering pails onto the platform, the girl stood between the preacher and matron, her sweet voice promising Jesus' love and forgiveness. When the hymn ended, the preacher's prayer thanked the Lord for the generosity of His people, He invited each who wanted to be saved or renew their faith to come forward and receive the Lord's blessing. To the haunting refrain of *Shall We Gather At The River,* I shuffled toward the angel, unable to hold back. I reached the platform amongst farmers and their women, overwhelmed by a smell of male sweat and perfumed soap.

The preacher placed his hand on the bowed head of a woman to my right. He was about to move on when I tugged his coat sleeve. He only patted my head. To my surprise, the angelic girl paused to gaze at me, smiled with dark red lips, touched her Bible to my head, and blessed me as the revival lady urged her along. The saved rabble returned to our benches. I gazed at my Keds to be sure I was on solid ground because I felt ready to fly. The dry grass and sawdust were real enough. Aunt Coletta hugged me and asked what I'd prayed for. My mind was on the angel but I told her I prayed Jarrold would be safe in the war. She cried, and I felt bad, because what I really longed for was to be with that girl forever.

If I slept that night it was in brief patches of dozing as my heart beat so fiercely I thrashed to release excess energy. Stupor led to visions of me walking through fields of wind-blown grass with the fair Thessalie Havenhurst holding my hand as if wading into infinite green time. During breakfast, Aunt Coletta studied me like a nurse. I tried to be casual, but ached to be away toward the holy tent that had revealed a new universe. I pictured the girl in sunlight, hair tasseled about her face by the breeze.

The revival field was bleak as I rounded Oberton Hardware toward the tent. I saw two dusty sedans parked behind, and a wood house trailer. Two men leaned on tent ropes sipping coffee from tin cups. They wore work pants and check shirts, sleeves rolled over muscular arms. They asked what I was after. I mumbled about wanting to help, but they shrugged and went back to talking and their coffee. I sat beside the tent out of the mid-morning sun till the preacher came out in his undershirt and pants, suspenders loose about his thighs like garter snakes. The boy who had played the bass drum followed behind.

They came over to the two men, chatted for a few minutes, and then the preacher waved me over and asked what I wanted. The boy with him stood my height, sandy hair cut low on his forehead so that he seemed to peer through grass. I told the preacher that he'd saved my soul and could I help his crusade? He was so tall it was hard not to be humble when he stared at me, hands on his hips. He asked if I was willing to do the Lord's work. Not sure what that might involve as I glanced at the trailer hoping to see the angel, I told him yes. He nodded, and the boy took me around back to a table with dirty dishes.

He said to help clear the table. We carried dishes and tin cups to a smaller table by a pail of sudsy water, dumped everything in, and I began scrubbing. I put the dishes on the table where they dried in the sun. I said my name was Robby. His was like 'Ep' or 'Ef' and left me puzzled till I finished up and the lady came in overalls that made her look fatter. She gave me a queer look and shrugged toward the boy before ambling to the coffee pot on an iron grill and pouring some in a cup I'd just washed.

She said her name was Sarah, Mrs. Judah Havenhurst, and asked why I was about. I said something about being saved. She shrugged, and when I asked about the boy, who had gone off into the big tent, she said his name was Eph, short for Ephesus. Surely I'd heard about Paul's letters to the Ephesians since I was a saved soul? A girl came out in a pink flower cotton blouse wearing jeans but barefoot as she sauntered toward me like a deer just awakened. Instead of cream white skin, she was as tan as a field hand, with short honey-blond hair, brown eyebrows, blue eyes, and a nose as freckled as her cheeks. She stretched, glanced at me, and then poured herself a cup of coffee.

They went into the tent without a word. I waited outside a while before going to gaze inside. The girl and her mom were sweeping the platform. Dust drifted through the shaded interior. I edged close to sneak glances, trying to find the angel, but I didn't and wondered if there was another girl still inside their trailer. The preacher sat on a wood chair studying the Bible and making notes in a small pad. The lady hummed. I asked if there was more to do. He said I could help Eph straighten the benches.

I said 'Hi' to Eph as I grabbed one end of a bench to align it. We worked silently until we'd finished one side of the tent. He went to the trailer and brought two bottles of root beer. We drank sitting in back, staring at the empty platform, and he said something strange: 'I hate this life.' He gulped his root beer, slowly shook his head, and sighed so mournfully I thought he might cry. I couldn't imagine how anyone hated moving around and having new experiences every day instead of staying in the same old place. I said that to him. He glared at me and mumbled, 'Christ.'

The lady and girl proceeded to rehearse that evening's program. The girl climbed the ramp and hid behind the curtain. Her mother sang the opening of a hymn and the girl came out slow like a doll, stiff-legged, both arms at her sides. The lady yelled and the girl folded her arms, went behind the curtain, and this time didn't come out when she should. Then the girl stuck her face out, smiled, and closed the curtain abruptly. The lady called to the preacher, who looked grim and stared into his Bible.

'What's wrong?' I asked the boy. He flung the root beer bottle aside. 'The little bitch is mad today,' he said. 'Sweet Thessalie Havenhurst, Angel of the Prairie.' After a long silence, I asked if she was named after a Bible book, too. He smiled and said with emphasis on every syllable, 'Thes-sa-lon-ians.' We straightened benches while I grew tired and sad. He asked in a whisper if I wanted to make some money. As we traipsed between the benches with gunnysacks retrieving trash, he helped me spot, and pocket, coins dropped during the revival. It was the way Eph got extra money. He picked up a lot; I got over two dollars in nickels, dimes and quarters.

When I left later that afternoon and returned home, Aunt Coletta wanted to know where I'd been. I said helping the Prairie Disciplers. She thought that was a holy thing to do, and when we'd done with supper and dressed for another night of revival, I was less keen than before. She gave me a quarter for the collection, which I dutifully dropped in the bucket. In spite of myself, I was still captivated by Thessalie in her robe and satin wig when she passed. I trembled with a desire to see her again, to study the odd girl who spent every daylight moment in silence.

That's what I did on Sunday, helping Eph, watching Thessalie, and finding coins to buy Eskimo Pies and Popsicles. The last meeting was that night, and after, when the group packed to leave, I made a last sweep of the interior picking up coins with Eph. He remained dour, but when we finished, he thanked me for helping. I wished him well just as Thessalie walked by dressed in her jeans. Impulsively, I wished her well, too. She stared through me and kept going. Eph shrugged with a sad smile. I hung around like a pitiful puppy hoping for attention while Thessalie sashayed through the tent kicking up dust with her bare feet. Empty-souled and disheartened, I trudged home, drenched in mystery. Some part of me was transfigured, but mostly I felt cursed with dry regret.

FAILURE IN KIND

There must've been some success. I'm not casting blame, yet Mother's first two marriages ended in divorce. The third teetered like a circus clown on a high wire with an umbrella. We moved to Badersville in California's central valley June 1944. Harmon worked in the oil fields. He wasn't subject to military service due to age--he was forty and also had a battered knee from high school football. A much-dissatisfied man, he did things on impulse. He braked the gray 1941 Plymouth on a dirt road one night to grab his shotgun and blast a jack rabbit held in the headlights. We had it broiled for supper. I hated the stringy meat and spitting-out lead buckshot. Deciding he'd never get ahead working for others, he opened a grocery.

It was located on the lower floor of our white, wood-frame house on Seventh Street. My bedroom was over the produce counter. The smell reminded me of rotting field crops--especially during hot summers. Harmon got up at five each day and went to the Cash-N- Carry Wholesale for meat, produce and package products. Unlike a man destined for failure, he was husky with a ready smile that crinkled both eyes as if he was amused by some joke. Mother looked serious, which taxed her pert prettiness so that she often appeared older than her thirty-five years.

The burlap curtained-off storeroom held boxes of goods we couldn't get onto the shelves. My job after school was to fill stock or pull cans forward so the shelves looked full. Harmon wanted the store to seem well-stocked even if rationing or our meager money limited selection more than the markets on the boulevard. Hard as we worked, we never got ahead. There was mind-numbing weariness in dusting, sweeping and cleaning. The meat case glass needed daily wiping inside and out. The large front window collected dust from the cotton and potato fields. I pinched brown edges off lettuce and cabbage so each head looked fresh, and rotated tomatoes or peaches to hide finger pokes. It was tedious, made worse by the idea that it was pointless. That's what gave me an attitude of futility years before I understood that the world didn't give a damn about my personal wellbeing.

There were compensations. While the war lasted, we never went without minor luxuries. When Harmon managed a rare box of Hershey bars, he set aside six before doling out the other eighteen to regular customers. But, daily life was very hand-to-mouth, aggravated by our eating whatever we couldn't sell. Even after the war ended in September 1945, we ate stale produce, brown meat, pulpy oranges, overripe bananas, dry apples, and wilted celery or carrots that my water spraying hadn't kept crisp. We used dented fruit and vegetable cans nobody bought.

My treat on Saturday; I could have anything in the store for lunch. I once heated a can of chili in a pan of water on the hot plate and wolfed it down with two bottles of Hires root beer and a pint of chocolate ice cream. Later, my gut exploded, and I put up with Harmon's disapproval for my inexcusable over-indulgence. I skipped our usual Saturday supper, an austere ritual of bread-and-milk that he'd had each week as a kid. He said it made him appreciate his blessings. Torn bread in a bowl of tepid milk made me nauseous. I held my breath to get it down.

When I was a high school freshman, doing average to no one's surprise and in dread of flunking Algebra and Spanish, holding on to the store became hard. During 1948 Badersville experienced a boom in supermarkets. Their grand openings were festooned with searchlights, bands, and lower prices. Our sales declined. Harmon drank more than his usual three jiggers of bourbon each night. A salesman's job for a wholesaler in Oakland came along. We saw him off on a bus one Sunday morning in spring 1949 for his interview on Monday.

He didn't come home, or telephone. Mother worried through Tuesday, while I skipped school to help in the store. Harmon returned Wednesday night, haggard, a purple bruise on his left cheek. They argued out of my hearing as I tried to complete homework. After an hour I gave up because their muted voices in the kitchen were more intriguing than social studies or biology. Harmon nursed a cup of black coffee. I got a glass of water and sat at the table. Without asking, I felt a right to learn about our situation. After his long bus ride and getting a room at the hotel in Oakland, he went for supper in a diner, then to a saloon for his evening bourbon. He fell in with three sailors. When the tab ran up, he offered to treat them to a bottle and drink cheaper in his room. Around midnight a fight broke out. It ended with the police.

Even though Harmon was innocent, he was taken to the station house. It was dawn before he was let out. When he got to the interview and explained, the food manager was sympathetic but stated he couldn't hire him under such circumstances. Harmon felt he'd only tried to be a good guy, and Mother agreed. I was suspicious. He became more determined to make a change. When my sophomore year ended, he sold the store and bought a more promising venture in Ojai, a town inland from Ventura. It was a small store, but with no supermarkets nearby. We moved in June and lived in a bungalow behind the store.

The work wasn't as demanding, but also didn't net enough to cover expenses. We stuck it out that summer while despair haunted us once more. Harmon sold the store to an elderly couple and we moved to Van Nuys in the San Fernando Valley. I started junior year while he got a job handling trading stamps colored money green. He drove every day, often Saturdays and Sundays, delivering stamps to stores and soliciting new accounts. Mother worked as a drug store cashier to make ends meet. I distributed stamp leaflets door-to-door for new stamp client gas stations, dry cleaners, or beauty salons. Stuffing them in screen doors was worse than clerking in a grocery. On an especially smoggy afternoon, I slacked off by sticking five leaflets in each doorway. People complained at the gas station. Harmon got bawled out for my laziness, another black mark on my work history.

The marriage deteriorated. Mother put up with his more frequent drinking, while Harmon nagged about her three-packs-a-day cigarette habit. I didn't like the smell of bourbon, and smoke irritated my hay fever. I couldn't concentrate in school. Nothing interested me. I embraced the futility of trying to accomplish anything, a normal adolescent cynicism aggravated by my home life. I got so miserable and angry that I fudged my age and joined the army the middle of June. The Korean War broke out a week later. My mother went berserk, screaming at me and Harmon. He lolled at the kitchen table with a drink, mumbled that military discipline would do me good; this from a drinker who hadn't been in the service or succeeded at anything. He wanted me out of the house to save money.

The two weeks before I left were a nightmare of warnings and recriminations. On the bus ride to Fort Ord I breathed the air of freedom. I was so enthused being on my own that the grind of basic training, which included blood blisters from KP and foot sores from marching, thrilled me. I became an artillery ammunition handler, delivered shells to gun crews, smoked without inhaling, and guzzled beer with my buddies. Two years later, after time in Japan and Korea, I felt in control of my life and released from the anguish that had driven me away from home.

I returned in 1952. They'd been divorced a year. Mother was dating. Harmon had lost the stamp job and delivered gas station supplies between Riverside and Las Vegas. He died when his car ran off the road in Nevada. Failure had dogged him to a tragic ending. I don't believe in fate. Life involves options and choices. But in quiet moments an eerie sensation overcomes me: bad luck plagues some lives. Are certain people doomed despite diligence and hard work? I've made mistakes and done foolish things, but avoided catastrophe-- thus far. I'm more anxious about this than I want to be, and can't shake the fear that, sooner or later, I'll come to grief.

DEMOLITION MAN

I was eleven in summer '44 when the magical power of blowing things up was revealed to me. Memory doesn't record where us kids found those explosive ingredients, but we did. Shotgun powder and percussion caps. We began with simple mischief; putting one-inch and three-inch firecrackers down anthills in the vacant lot behind our subdivision. Badersville on hot, dusty days had a way of turning curious boyish indolence into dangerous behavior. The valley was planted in cotton, potatoes, and sugar beets amid foothills with a forest of creosoted timber oil derricks staunch as sentinels across the alkali fields.

If the Devil finds work for idle hands, he also opens the ears to temptation. It was at supper one night when, only half listening, I caught the comment from Mom that ants were invading her kitchen. Dad mumbled that he'd have to do something about it when he got time. There were, to my amazement, anthills in our own backyard, and they were causing trouble. As I prowled the next day, sure enough, there they were. Not large, but menacing nonetheless. When

I conveyed my find to the gang, we found the insects in their back yards as well. We went to war against the invaders with leftover firecrackers and delighted in not only satisfying our lust for destruction, but also helping our parents.

Eventually, as we discovered larger anthills and longed to raise the blast level to heights of explosive delight, we began using bigger firecrackers stuffed into the anthill, and for greater damage, pouring a quantity of shotgun powder into the hole. The firecracker acted as a fuse or primer, setting off the powder. Dirt flew, leaving a crater. This was so exciting that I made the mistake of telling about it at supper one night. My dad asked questions, listened till I mentioned the shotgun powder, and then bawled me out for using such dangerous stuff and don't do it ever again. I had to promise that I wouldn't. He said he'd contact somebody to take care of the ants using a strong poison.

It seems strange to remember that my dad's bawling me out could cause loss of sleep, but it did. Not so much because of what he said. I had been chastised before. The idea that bothered me most was telling the others I couldn't blow up anthills anymore. If they went ahead anyway I'd be left out of the only exciting summer activity. When we met, they planned more blasts with shotgun powder and, also, Bullseye pistol powder. One of the dads reloaded ammo for sport and target practice, so the group was amply supplied with ordnance for blasting ants by the millions. I said that not only couldn't I participate, but that they couldn't do it in my back yard.

There was nothing about not being able to tag along, however. So we scrounged around and, by chance, came upon an enormous anthill in a neighbor's yard behind his garage. It looked heaven-sent. Nearly as big as a garbage can lid, it rose almost half a foot high and had an opening two or three inches wide with ants entering and exiting through a dozen tiny gullies they had worn into the loose alkali soil. We all stared at this massive fortress and were stunned by its challenge. No giant firecracker or shotgun powder seemed likely to do it justice. That's when we contrived, with my help, to make a major project out of obliterating it. We agreed that Bullseye pistol powder was the explosive of choice, but we had to find a way to make it more lethal.

When a plan emerged, it was, in retrospect, ingenious. First, it was decided that we must use the whole can of powder. A steel rod was found in one boy's garage. Using a hand mallet,

we pounded the steel rod into the ground as close to the anthill opening as we dared, and as deep as we could drive it. We took turns pounding the rod. The ants, realizing they were under attack, crawled up our legs. We had to stop and brush them off before we got bitten. Eventually the rod was two feet down and only a foot or so sticking up. We worked like slaves to loosen it enough so it could be pulled out, leaving a cylindrical hole an inch across.

Into this crevice, feeling like miners preparing to blast gold ore from granite, we poured the entire can of Bullseye pistol powder. It disappeared into the hole, so much so that we didn't even see any. The boy who'd brought it said maybe he could find some more if he went home and looked again. He left while the rest of us got Nehi Orange and Hires Root Beer in bottles and guzzled. It occurred to me as we sat there that we were real close to the back of the neighbor's garage wall, which had a small square window in the middle divided into four parts by a wood lattice. If Mr. Mundt gazed out that window, he would see five of us sitting lazy and innocent, but staying as far back from the bustling anthill as we could against the fence. When the boy got back with a second can of powder it, too, almost disappeared down the bottomless hole. But this time the last of the powder, dangerous-looking in its grainy texture, was just visible a few inches from the top.

I remember sweating as we talked about how to fire it off, finally deciding to use the last of our firecrackers--a three-inch salute that, if placed under an empty Crisco can, would hurl it a hundred feet into the sky. The salute was tamped into the hole. We were so excited we trembled. If we'd had any notion of what was about to happen, we'd have quivered with fright. Much talk followed about who should have the privilege of lighting the fuse. It took a series of coin tosses before it fell to me. Recalling Dad's warning, it didn't seem that I could be punished for an act determined by mere chance. I struck three matches before my shaky fingers didn't snuff the flame out. As the fuse flared, I lunged near the crouched others ten feet from the anthill.

As it turned out, that wasn't far enough. I don't recall the explosion. There was a hot, stinging sensation, along with a rush of air that sucked my lungs dry. Neighbor ladies claimed later that they thought a bomb had exploded. After I sat up, having been knocked over, the first thing visible was alkali dust that rained down like tan snow. Mr. Mundt's garage window was blown out. Boys on either side moved their lips, shouted, but their voices sounded hollow. The twitching bodies of large black ants settled into my palm. The air was filled with falling ants. I thought they were flying. Queen ants could fly, but was the entire anthill full of queens?

Mr. Mundt, the retired navy officer, came around the corner of his garage, looked grim and puzzled at the half dozen of us sprawled in the grass covered with dust and dead or dying ants. The anthill was gone, replaced by a hole. He asked if any of us were hurt, but we couldn't hear the words. I shook my head, more out of stunned bravado. For all I knew at that instant I might be near death. When clear that nobody was injured, and we leaned against the fence, it came to me that the air reeked of burnt powder. It must be the odor of a battlefield, something never experienced just watching a war movie. Mr. Mundt herded us around his garage into the shade of his back porch and went in to fetch glasses and a pitcher of cherry Kool-Aid.

While lounging, we all noticed the ants, huge black ants everywhere. That's when we knew that we hadn't destroyed the anthill so much as simply flung ants everywhere. I saw ants in the grass and flower beds, also on the walls of nearby houses. It was catastrophic.

All six of us were blasted by our parents. We had to surrender allowances and spending money to pay for a man to come with a poison called Cyno-Gas. It was poured down anthills to kill them without bombast or horrific side-effects. During the Korean War I became a combat engineer, one of the guys who managed explosives. I felt right at home. Blasting bunkers with quarter pound TNT bricks was a return to childhood. The world, it seemed, could always find useful work for those with latent destructive tendencies.

WADING DEEP MEMORY

H ate is supposed to be bad for health, so recalling how much hatred has been part of one's life has to be a drain on my mental state--right? But of course, it hasn't been only that. I mean, every memory is a grab bag of terrific and terrible. I'm not exceptional. But my situation is unique, if I may say so. It relates not merely to childhood but specific events in the summer of 1944 when I was eleven. Mother and me left our modest life in Fargo for hot, arid Badersville in California's central valley. It was wartime and a contagious frenzy pervaded the dry climate and endless days of one-hundred-plus temperature. We'd come west so she could marry Ancil Shields, a former high school beau, and forget my dad confined to a VA hospital mental ward in Bismarck.

This isn't the time to get into all of that stuff. It's enough for you to know that my dad was paranoid-schizo-something-or-other with complications so weird that even the doctors didn't understand it. What sticks in my mind are episodes of drunken mayhem sufficiently bizarre that even today they seem more like movie scenes than actual events.

Mother was slapped around, and I got more spankings than any other kid with a natural talent for mischief. From age five through nine I thought most fathers must be like that-- moody, absorbed, with wild episodes of anger for no reason. It was only after he was sent to the nut house after much fuss getting doctors to sign him in, and we roomed with a middle-aged couple whose kids had already left home, that I witnessed normal family life. Gazing back on our California move, I guess Mother was trying to do her best for us. That Ancil would be bad in his own weird way came as a shock.

Due to problems from a high school football injury that gave him a limp, he was exempt from military service. Ancil was three years older than my mother at thirty-eight, medium height with huge arms and a brawny chest. His sandy hair was combed straight back despite a receding hairline. He had a pocked face but was good-looking in a kind of manly way. When he smiled it appeared genuine, skin crinkling at the corners of his blue-gray eyes. He worked as a foreman in the field of Perce County Oil Company. One day he took me with him when he toured various drilling sites in the valley and nearby foothills. It seemed like an important job for the war effort but that didn't keep things from going haywire.

For one thing--Ancil drank. Often more than my dad used to. And when he got drunk on Saturday night sitting at the kitchen table with Mother while they smoked and sloshed bourbon over ice, Ancil got surly. Quite weird, really, how a man who was even-tempered and cordial sober could turn into such a belligerent bastard after half a dozen shots of booze. But there it was. My mother tried to hold him back. When that didn't work she put more ice cubes and tap water in his glass. That led to mindless bickering and shouting that kept me awake till he wore down and she coaxed him to bed. He didn't get up Sundays until after noon, then sat somberly reading the newspaper all day.

HUNCHING HOMEWARD

Mother gave no excuses for Ancil or apologized for the way things started to go crazy-- I'll give her that. She made lots of mistakes in life and accepted the blame without complaint. If she felt more than a fair share of bad luck had come her way, she never said so. There were times when I watched her alone at the kitchen table, smoking as she thumbed through a magazine with a faraway look, not seeing each page before she turned it, often with thin tears streaking her face. I never had a chance to hate Dad before he was out of my life. But Ancil...well. Within weeks of arriving in Badersville a rage began to swell inside of me like a malignant growth. I'd never felt that way before so it was both frightening and enjoyable. It occupied my thoughts every day because as a new kid in the area there was little to do. The days were hot as blazes, withering leaves on oaks, elms and poplars until they twisted like sun-dried worms. I kept myself inside under the swamp cooler to avoid heatstroke. Before I knew what was happening I'd created a full-time hate for Ancil's loutishness. I considered him a sonofabitch, relishing the forbidden epithet that legitimized my entry into adult expression.

The upsetting thing was, it didn't always go bad. Ancil could be a nice guy. We went fishing for bass on the Perce River with some buddies from the oil company. They puffed cigars and cigarettes, cursed and joked in English and Mexican, guzzled cold beer for hours, and didn't get drunk. I learned all about bait, rods and reels, so it was an okay time. Then there was squirrel and gopher hunting, with the guys and some of their kids. Ancil had a single shot .410 shotgun he let me use, teaching gun safety, aiming, cleaning and such. That was okay, too. But Saturday nights--the booze. By August, it went beyond just yelling. I heard him hit something, the table maybe, but when I went to the kitchen for a glass of water, Mother held a hand to her cheek and didn't look at me. I got a sour-gut tremble.

Then there were the beatings. I don't think I was naughty, but when a smarty neighbor boy gave me a girlie magazine, I kept it under my pillow. Mother found it and Ancil lectured me on right and wrong, then walloped my butt until I had blood welts that leaked onto my briefs. One day, idle and bored, I drew the sketch of a man peeing into a bucket. It was silly and made me laugh. Ancil saw it on my desk, asked if that was the way my mind worked, the filthy ideas I had. That led to another session with the thick leather belt. I didn't resent being punished. For all I knew my faults were awful. But later he acted more interested in hurting me than making me a better person. He, in my most dire thoughts, was out to get me.

Looking back, I had a vivid and a morbid imagination. I wondered what would happen, for example, if Ancil ever got drunk while fishing from the wooden skiff on the river and fell in. It was a lazy river, but the reddish-brown water moved resolutely down the valley with swirls and eddies. It was possible that a man lacking control of himself might drown. Or a shooting accident. While hunting we were careful to break open the breeches of shotguns clambering through barbed wire fences. Just knowing guns were lethal added possibilities. To my way of thinking, I felt justified protecting myself from a menace.

On Labor Day we joined a group of families from the oil company for a picnic at Perce County Park near the river. Wooden tables, big salads, burgers and hot dogs on grills prevailed. Mother and I had only been in Badersville for three months. It seemed years and, worse, that it would go on forever. The European war news after the D-Day landings no longer fascinated me, nor did movies or reading. Starting school the next day was even less on my mind. I felt trapped, and realized that Mother, having already failed in two grim marriages, had trapped us in another dismal situation. I recalled my first stepdad's .38 Special pistol that he'd used as a railway mail clerk and wondered if she still had it hidden away someplace.

I carried the full weight of my discontent toward Ancil. Rather than imagining evil things happening to him, it crept into my mind that I should think of ways to escape. I could run away, hit the road, ride the rails--in retrospect wildly unreal behavior that would have failed and led to even deeper despair. Adults, and kids splashed in the murky river shallows. Because I didn't feel like lingering with the adults, and still didn't know any kids very well, I waded into the river by myself, the tepid flow near shore sluicing my prickly hot skin.

As I wandered farther out and the pebbles under my feet gave way to a soft, oozing silt that slimed above my ankles, the chilling idea hit me that maybe there was quicksand. I pictured the melodramatic demise of a vicious Nazi in a Tarzan movie. He was led into quicksand and sucked beneath it while grasping at nearby vines to save himself. I looked about but saw nothing to clutch. I approached the river easing past the pool that had been created by a protective cove for picnickers. My reverie envisioned a raft to drift down river, like Huckleberry Finn, floating me away, leaving my mother and Ancil, and everything else that I disliked, behind. My brain flooded with images of indolent escape. The sun beat down on scalp and neck as I ventured out from under the shadows of the oaks, elms and cottonwoods.

I didn't look back, afraid to notice anyone watching me, equally concerned if nobody cared whether I wandered off or not. Water swirled around my waist as it deepened. I stepped with utmost care, each bare foot sinking into muddy silt that seeped between my toes, making my heart pound while I trembled and sank deeper until I feared being sucked under. It was an uncommon sensation, toying with life, tempting danger--savoring the brute reality on the outer edge of something truly momentous, an adult experience. In those seconds I felt actually alive, ready to learn what life was all about. It meant raw peril and thrills, not the trivia of boozing and arguing. It was about living, and daring. The water reached my chest, but I was secure against the current with both feet anchored in muck.

I hesitated to take another step but, overcome by an urgency to tempt fate, I stepped out. My left foot felt nothing beneath it. I didn't fall forward, or even slide downward--I plummeted straight into blackness. So sudden was the lunge that I gasped, convulsed, and swallowed gulps of acidic water. Then I choked and flung my arms out and up, trying to reach air, grasping for anything. But I couldn't rise. I surged along in the fierce flood and panicked, wondering how deep I'd go before touching the beckoning bottom. In stupidity I thought I'd sink down and ease up its steep, sucking bank into shallower water. Where the hell was it? My feet sought the mud below, but liquid space suspended me like a puppet. I flailed, unaware that the pain in my arms wasn't the river's grip but human hands.

Someone dragged me into shallow water. I heard grunts, shouting, women squealing. I coughed brackish water. My nostrils burned. Both ears were plugged, every sound a drumbeat. Carried onto dry ground, I was wracked by the awkward, jerking motion of whoever held me. I gazed up into Ancil's face while he lugged me to a group near the picnic table. He laid me on a blanket, his short sleeve shirt glued to his body like cotton skin, and slapped my face so hard I yelled 'sonofabitch!' Men laughed and said 'kid's gonna be okay.'

I became the celebrity of the picnic gathering, much to my shame. Everybody wanted to know why I had gone out so far. Didn't I know it was treacherous? Folks made excuses because I was new in town. Ancil received slaps on the back while he swilled beers. His right foot had been gashed so deep by a rock that it took an hour to staunch the bleeding. The damnedest thing, for the rest of the day he never looked at me. It was as if I didn't exist and my almost drowning involved only him. Mother cried, hugging him. I felt more alone than ever.

I was too stunned to be grateful and found, to my humiliation, that I resented him more. Not for saving me but for being less hate-able. I had to rebuild my hatred of him and managed it. Of course, I didn't leave home, at least not right away. He remained the person he was. So did I. He continued to booze and rage. I coped until leaving at seventeen. People don't change even if they've had rough experiences forced deep inside them. It was a rotten time in my life and hasn't been a lot better since. There, now. I've told you about the hating.

Same time next week--right?

BAD INFLUENCE

I spend so much time scanning the brush-covered hills and gullies, glancing ahead and behind for Lutey, that I'm almost undone by catastrophe. The moment of sheer terror is a pulsating memory that hasn't faded in fifty years: I'm flat on my back with sagebrush pressed against my T-shirt. The sky is pale and vast, my legs quivering encased in well-worn Levis. Every aspect of my thirteen-year-old self is paralyzed by buzzing that bores into my brain like a drill. *Rattlesnake!*

Despite the dread that throbs close to my face, I can't summon the will to flee, and stay frozen as the blistering sun marinates my face with fear-sweat. Both hands clutch the Remington .22 caliber bolt-action rifle across my chest as though I am valiantly protecting--what? After more pounding seconds than I can measure, I sense the rattling is not next to my head but below, near my feet encased in boots. I rise up, trying to suppress a fierce heartbeat as nausea surges into my tight dry throat.

There it is: coiled, its tail a perpendicular blur of rattling menace. It's farther from my boots than I feared, maybe two feet, at the edge of the rabbit path I followed. Instinctively, I'd leaped to the higher side of the path. Without thought, gasping, I fire six shots so fast the rifle is emptied in seconds, tiny brass casings flying in the sunlight like gold insects. The rattlesnake twists in its death throes until it ceases to twitch and curls pale yellow belly up against a gnarled juniper. More minutes cascade through me before my legs are steady enough to stand. I gaze at the dragon I've slain and am filled with an adrenaline rush and queasiness.

I've been farmed out for two weeks of mid-summer '46 to my stepfather's friends on an oil-lease near Saugus in drear hills north of Los Angeles---Jack and Myra Tregasi. They're an elder rustic couple lacking children and have welcomed me with the heartiness of people who yearn for company without quite knowing how to relax around kids. They constantly ask after my wellbeing. Their two-bedroom house squats like a package left in the wilderness. A dozen grasshopper oil pumps chuff nearby. Jack's duties take him into Gulf Oil's dry hills perfumed with petroleum and chaparral.

I've the run of the hills and can shoot rabbits and gophers as long as my .22 caliber ammo holds out. Because I'm not much of a shot, I've contented myself acting like a western scout or Indian fighter. With my war surplus web belt and army canteen, along with a sheathed hunting knife, it's easy to play somebody more stalwart. After first arriving two days before, Jack and Myra warned me only to watch out for someone called Lutey--Myra talking like a fusty school marm. Jack, more stolid but with a crinkly smile, said she was making it more a worry than it was. I didn't know what to make of the warning because it sounded like Lutey was a bum who camped out in the hills and scrounged. The first time I ventured out, protected by my straw hat and trusty rifle, I sensed Lutey might be watching from every sagebrush gully like a renegade savage; but I soon forgot about him to stalk rabbits and gophers.

Now as I stare at the dead rattlesnake, it seems that I've accomplished something. I have killed. With care, I poke the snake with the rifle barrel, and then scoop it up like a slimy rope to carry from the dense brush. I make my way along the path before veering upward at an angle toward a clearing. Still weak from the stunning encounter, I toss the snake into dry grass and sit to swig from the canteen. I'm sitting back to the sun gazing at the snake, thinking I'll cut off the rattle as a souvenir, when brush crackles behind. A gritty voice makes my heart jump.

"Got yaself one, did ya, huh?"

"Yeahhh," I mutter, twisting.

I expect a man, ugly, brooding, with the evil demeanor of an outcast--the vagabond Lutey that Jack and Myra have cautioned me about. But it's not a man at all. Above in shadow with the sun in my face, stands a lanky youth in overalls, barefoot, bony arms and shoulders, ankles and feet alkali-brown with toes that appear to be clawing the ground. He has both hands tucked in his pockets and sidles past downslope till turning to peer back at me. He nudges the rattler with a big toe; that makes me shiver. It might be live enough to strike, but is inert under his prod.

"Right good size," he says, isolating the tail and rattle.

"Uh huh." My voice is dry despite gulps of water.

"Seen bigger uns, though."

"Me, too," I brag.

"You wan' the rattle?"

"Not sure. Yeah, maybe."

"Figgers." He looks down the slope. "Get two bits for it from the oil lease man."

"Oh, how come?"

"Way things is."

When he looks my way sort of gazing up the slope, I see he isn't older at all. In fact, he looks younger than me, thin-faced, sallow, but tan like leather, with a thatch of mustard colored hair uncombed around each pointed ear. His eyes, staring past, or perhaps through me, are almost golden green, like lizards pictured in *National Geographic*. His lips are the reddest I've ever seen and open just enough to let his words out. He appears such a natural part of the landscape that I feel like an intruder confronting the rightful inhabitant.

"I'm Robert Kalmer," I say.

He shrugs. "Luther Harding."

He takes a step toward me and I tense, gripping the canteen tight when I screw the cap back on. The rifle is cradled in my lap. He doesn't seem concerned. I put the canteen into its canvas pouch, take out my knife and, stepping on the rattler's head with one boot, lift the tail and cut off the rattle. I study it as if I've done it many times before, counting aloud the number of rattles: nine. He watches, nods as if it's his place to approve my kill. I gaze at the snake's red-brown scaled blotches, feeling eerily detached from everything.

"Looks to be an old one," I say, feigning casualness.

"Mebbe four, five years. Figger two rattles a year."

"Oh?" That is news. "How long do they live?"

"Got me some rattles twenty or more long."

"What kind of rattlesnake is this?"

"Pacific. Lotsa Panamints, Mojaves about."

"Well, guess I'd better be getting along."

"Ya livin' in the lease house?"

"Uh huh. The Tregasi's."

"You kin to 'em?"

"Nope."

"Mind I walk with ya?"

I shrug and start back down the rabbit trail, trying to recall how far I've wandered from the house. For a few anxious seconds all the hills ahead appear the same to me, and I can't be sure which one overlooks the Tregasi's house. I lope ahead of him, and haven't gone fifty yards when I halt, breathless once again. Stretched across the trail lies another rattlesnake. I hold the rifle tight in both hands, fearful as I try to discern which side of the brush trail conceals the head. I'm anxious about the boy waiting behind as I struggle over what to do. Finally, I kick a few dirt clods toward the snake. So fast that it startles me, the snake coils together in its strike posture, head poised in the S-shape of its forward length. I steady the rifle to take aim this time. Before I can shoot, a bony hand grips my shoulder.

"Don' hafta do that 'less ya wanta," he says.

"What do you mean? It's blocking the trail."

He eases past to the snake, which rears back buzzing with frenzy, and crouches as much as his lanky frame allows till he is only two or three feet from the rattler. Finding a gnarled scrub branch, he edges closer. The snake slithers back till pressed against the root of a chaparral and unable to retreat farther. The boy moves closer, presses the branch down on its neck, grabs and lifts it up until its tail clears the ground, and tosses the branch away. He gathers up the rest of the snake to cradle in his arms like a writhing baby while grasping the head with his right hand. Mumbling to the snake, he fingers the rattles that are longer than the one I killed.

"Wanta hold 'im?" he asks me.

"Huh uh," I say with a shudder.

"Won' hurtcha long's I hold 'im."

I reach out to touch the twisting body in its middle. I wrap my fingers around as far as they will stretch and only enclose half its girth. The slick, contorting body fills me with a sensation of raw life, flesh not constrained by sentiment or reflection, making me aware for the first time of the true meaning of *serpent*.

"It's a good 'un," he says with calm appraisal, studies the tongue-flicking head up close as he gazes right into its eyes, and then walks into the brush along the lower side of the trail to release the snake. It coils and rattles till, sensing that danger is past, glides into the brush. "Be long gone now 'cause a the scare we give 'im."

"Jeez," I say, "it sure was an awful strong one."

"Not the biggest, though. Lots bigger 'round here."

I scan the brush, which now appears as if it will engulf me in its tangled web with hundreds of rattlesnakes. The afternoon sun beats on my shoulders and arms, and my face is drenched with stinging sweat. I have been humbled by the boy's frontier skill and want to be away to restore my self-esteem. Three hawks circle, gliding before they swoop as if stalking prey. The boy, hands on hips, sniffs the air.

"Can smell 'em," he says. "Sun burns 'em up."

I don't understand that, but nod as though I do.

We continue along the trail, down one slope, across the shade side of another, and in half an hour stand on the hill above the Tregasi's house. I think about the rattle in my Levis pocket. It means nothing to me now. I give it to him. He studies it before shoving it in his overalls pocket. He can get a quarter for it, which I don't want or need. I unload the rifle; it's not good to enter a house with a loaded gun. Before I start downhill to the lease, he pats me on the shoulder.

"Most times I'm called Lutey."

"Yeah, I know. I'm Robby."

"See ya."

"Uh huh."

I've only gone maybe a dozen or twenty steps downward when I look back. He's already gone, probably down the far side of the hill. It doesn't surprise me when I think maybe he can just vanish into the wilderness, like a real Indian scout. I stomp inside the screened back porch and kick off my boots.

Myra brings me a glass of lemonade. She's my mother's age but seems more grandmother-like in her flower-print cotton dress and graying hair swirled into a bun. She wants to know if I've gotten any rabbits or gophers. I tell about the snake I shot, but not the other across the trail. Did I meet up with anybody? It's a strange question after wandering bleak, hills. Suddenly I realize that she's already seen Lutey and me before I traipsed down to the house.

"Yeah, Ma'am. I met a young boy roaming around."
She nods, pinches her lips. "That had to be Lutey."
"Sure, I think that's who it was all right."
"We warned you about him, didn't we?"
"I thought you were talking about a man."
"Lutey's just like a man. Wild and weird acting."
"He kills snakes, and sells the rattles to Mr. Tregasi."
"Humpf!" Myra folds her arms. "Weird, just the same."
"Where does he live? There aren't any houses nearby."
"Back a ways, farther on the lease. A shack with his pa."
"He doesn't seem like such an awful person."
"Mind, he's an odd one to keep away from."
"I don't expect to come across him again anyway."
"Just the same, your folks mean for us to look after you."

Jack Tregasi comes home before suppertime. Myra tells him about Lutey and me. He chuckles and brings out the rattle I've given away. Without a word he takes it onto the back porch and puts it in a Mason jar filled with rattles. That's when I see three other jars filled as well. I ask about them. He explains that he's killed some, but most he got from Lutey. The kid's not good for much, but he sure can kill rattlesnakes and helps keep the pump stations clear so roustabouts and oil field workers don't get bitten. During supper Myra repeats that I've spent time with Lutey and tells Jack to warn me away from the boy. He does, without conviction while Myra carries on about Lutey's bad influence. I don't get why she's

HUNCHING HOMEWARD

so down on him, and put out of my mind even as I promise her I won't spend time with the 'snake boy.'

During the rest of my stay, I meet Lutey in the hills. He traps rabbits for him and his dad. He's been bitten by rattlers, but is 'mune' to their poison. He shows me how to catch and handle them. I don't like it, but learn well enough to perform a useful service years later. Riding my bike in Palos Verdes on a Saturday, I see a rattlesnake slither toward a kids' baseball outfield. I find a stick to pin the snake, pick it up, and tote it into the wild. Lutey would've been proud. I told him he was said to be a bad influence. He didn't know about 'fluence' but 'figgered' I was probably 'mune. He was right; I've avoided most evil except life itself.

THE WAREHOUSE

"**M**aybe they're aliens," Marcus proclaimed in a breathless whisper.
Marcus was our expert on space invaders ever since he and his dad sighted flying saucers over Badersville that 1947 summer. Three of us fourteen-year-olds were on the weed slope near the brick building beside the railroad tracks. Switch engines belched steam, giving the night an eerie stink proper for monsters that might eat our faces.

"They look like regular folks," I said, uneasy anyway. "Ladies mostly."

"Fer cripes sakes, Robby!" Marcus said. "What about the fat guy?"

"Yeah," Berk said. He had thick glasses and hated his name, Berkeley.

I'd forgotten about the stocky man with a black fedora and overcoat who came in early evening carrying a leather satchel. He arrived at eight or nine each night, and didn't leave till twelve. In sunlight the building looked dull with metal-latticed windows, hardly a domain for flying saucer aliens. Some ladies walked to the steel door of the warehouse and tapped several times before it opened. Others arrived in cars that shut off headlights entering the deserted street. Most of the time only two people went in, usually women, sometimes a man and woman. When three showed up, it was one man and two women. Marcus, Berk, and me sensed we'd stumbled on a sinister place.

Another peculiar thing--the fat man with the satchel always came in a large black sedan. We called him 'The Boss.' He left last. When others left, one woman had to be helped because she seemed lame or weak. The third week of watching we moved beyond morbid curiosity into thinking we'd discovered a dangerous situation. We argued about telling our folks and decided that would mean explaining where we spent our summer nights when we were supposed to be staying at each other's house.

"Let's get closer," Marcus said, suggesting we creep down to a window with gray light spilling onto stacked railroad ties. Berk and me held back. Marcus said, "It might be nothing. We'd be durn fools to report and get ourselves in trouble to boot."

That was sensible, but as Marcus led us down the slope after a girl, who looked to be not much older than we were, went in with a man, Berk and me let him go ahead. The window glass was frosted. Marcus squinted through a crack. I heard a man's voice, and a woman crying, sort of muffled like a child holding a kerchief over her mouth.

Marcus turned away from the window, looking ashen in the yellowed light. Berk didn't want to look, but I squeezed close, shut my left eye, and peeked. I noticed a white sheet stretched as if on a clothesline, and smelled medicine-stink, iodine maybe; it made my nostrils itch. Then I heard gushing, running water, and sensed that a toilet was being flushed. We scooted back to our place and waited till a man and girl came out a half hour later. She leaned against him, moaning. Before getting to the car she went limp and would've fallen if he hadn't picked her up in his arms. After laying her in the back seat, he drove off, tires flinging gravel. It came to me like a sudden chill: no matter why the women came, somebody was hurting them.

"We have to call the police," Marcus said.

Now Berk spoke up, worried. "But what for?"

"Because." Marcus added, "They might be crooks, or communists."

That put a scare into me. "Communists?"

"Sure. They're out to destroy us. My dad said so. And this is a perfect hideout…."

His words hung in the dark night. We concluded that an anonymous phone call was best. Marcus had the deepest voice, so he'd call from the pay booth at the Gulf gas station. I admit to trembling when he dialed; Berk shifted from foot to foot.

"Yes, uh, sir," Marcus began. "I'd like to report, uh, some dangerous activity." He went silent for a moment. "I'd rather not say, sir. It's just that people are acting mighty strange at the train yard… Yeah, I mean, yes, in the big old warehouse." There was a long pause. He glanced at us, and then said, "Things seem suspicious with folks, ladies, going in and out each night."

"I should be getting home," Berk exclaimed in a rush.

"Quiet!" I said as Marcus covered the mouthpiece.

"Uh, that wasn't nobody," Marcus said into the phone. "I was thinking about getting on home. No, I won't be here when you check it out. No, sir, that's not what I want to do… huh, uh…goodbye." He hung up fast. "Let's scram outta here."

"Why?" Berk wailed. "What's wrong?"

"I don't know," Marcus said, hurrying down the street with Berk and me behind trying to keep up. "We'd just better skedaddle."

To get home we had to pass the warehouse. We were running as a police car sped up behind. I almost wet my pants. Car doors opened; a gruff voice turned me into a statue.

"Hold it, you damned kids!"

"Holy cripes!" Berk squawked.

God, they looked huge in their tan uniforms, chests and bellies, leather and badges and revolvers, billy clubs. Both wore campaign hats and aviator sunglasses even though it was almost midnight. The cop next to Marcus took off his glasses and stared at us. I liked it better when his eyes were hidden. We looked pitiful in our jeans and T-shirts.

"Which one of you phoned?" the biggest growled at Marcus.

"Me, sir," Marcus said, his voice not nearly as grownup as he had pretended on the phone. "I'm the one that, uh... called....sort of."

"About that building over there?" the officer said, pointing.

"Yes, sir, that's the one. We were merely wandering by--"

"How long you been hanging around here at night?"

"Well." Marcus glanced at us. "Couple nights."

"More'n that, I'd say," the second cop remarked, nodding to the first. "I'd betta call it in, loiterin'. We goin' ta lock 'em up for tha night?"

"Wait a sec," the first said, staying on Marcus. "What is it you think's going on?" When Marcus shrugged, the cop said, "I got all night, son. Take your time."

"Don't know for sure," Marcus said. "Just seems weird. Folks in and out. Lots of ladies, that's all. We thought maybe, you know, bootleggers or criminals."

"Bootleggers?" The second cop smirked. "Jeez, they went out with FDR."

"Come on, boys," the first said, including me and Berk in a look with a thin-lipped grin. "You can do better than that. Let's have it."

"We thought they might be flying saucer aliens!" Berk exclaimed.

"Now why'n hell would ya think that?" the second cop said, chuckling.

"Because of the fat man with the black satchel," I said, as flustered as Berk.

"What about him?" the first said, a harsh tone now. When none of us spoke, he put a big hand on Marcus' shoulder. "You! Talk!"

"Just a fat guy with a black bag." The first cop glanced at the other, and nodded, then glared at Marcus, who felt a need to talk some more. "We call him The Boss."

For a silent few moments the first cop gazed into the street, his face serious in the glow of the only streetlight high above the turn-in to the warehouse. Then he put his arm around Marcus and escorted us to the squad car while the other walked ahead, reached in for the radio mike, and began talking. He mumbled some stuff about 'three kids' and 'the mill' and 'Doc Skozik' while the first folded his arms and watched us. The one on the radio was jovial, laughed, slapped his belly. He signed off, winked at the first officer.

"Now look, kids. Got na business down here at night, see? What's goin' on over there's got nothin' ta do with aliens. Understand?"

"Sure we do," Berk said, nodding like a puppet.

"What about ya?" the second one asked me.

I shuffled my tennies in the gravel, remembering the peculiar smell from the room that had almost made my eyes water, like they now seemed about to on their own. Maybe it was the recollection of the young girl, the way she walked, the wounded bird sound she emitted heading for the car, and the way she collapsed. I didn't look at either cop as I thought things out, but the second one kept after me, his lips moving while my ears blocked out what he was saying. My gut gurgled and I felt as if it might get the runs; the last thing I wanted was to mess myself.

"I'm askin' ya one las' time," the officer repeated.

I looked off, but blurted, "A girl got hurt in there."

"And jus' how'n hell ya know that, son?"

The first one said to Marcus, "We can do this two ways. Drive you home in the squad car and tell your folks what you've been doing. Or, let you go now, and we don't see you here ever again. What'll it be?"

That sounded easy, and Berk was already leaning to get going. Marcus gave me a look, then shrugged. We opted to scoot home as fast as we could. For the last days of that summer we discussed it in hushed voices, then let go as we got busy as freshmen in high school. It was a year later I read in the newspaper about the warehouse being raided in a crime cleanup. What was really going on in there wasn't made clear in the article, which had a lot more to say about shutting down gambling dens and betting parlors. But I have my suspicions to this day, and I know for sure that it wasn't space aliens.

PATCHWORKING

I didn't find out about Harmon and the other woman until Monday after the big Saturday night fight. My mother, Livy, and her third husband were often at each other, especially when he was drinking. The front door of the flat-roofed bungalow behind our neighborhood grocery store slammed, the gray 1941 Plymouth engine growled to life, and the rumble faded into the Ojai night. Harmon stayed away all day Sunday. Mom called my grandmother, Ida, at the Christian Science Home and she arrived for a stay to lament Livy's smoking and drinking.

It was mid-July 1949, between my sophomore and junior years in high school. Monday morning I scrounged a bowl of Cheerios before noticing the car beside the store. I didn't have to go to my job at Mrs. Bender's restaurant till five, so I went into the back of the store to sweep, dust, and wipe the meat counter glass, refrigerated cabinet and freezer. I restocked canned goods from the dark storeroom or pulled cans forward to make every item appear fully stocked. Even though the store smelled of vegetables, fruit, and meat, the strongest scent was mustiness and sootiness from hillside fires the year before that left the locale with crusty oaks looking ragged and forsaken.

Ida came in with the cash box and sorted change into the register. She was in her blue flower print dress with a white dishtowel for an apron. Milk and dairy goods would be delivered, but I didn't know what we'd do about produce if Harmon didn't go to the Cash-N-Carry. When I asked Ida, she said Livy would take care of it. At half past nine, after three or four customers had come and gone for bread and milk, Livy entered, her eyes red as she daubed her cheeks with a handkerchief. She had found Harmon passed out in the back seat of the car, a woman's wet bathing suit on the floor. Ida hugged her for a bit, said soothing things I didn't hear, and then Livy left to get produce.

She was gone most of the morning while Ida kept apologizing to local ladies who asked about fruit and vegetables. There was fussing and head shaking about poor service. When Livy returned at noon, she didn't have any produce. She had spent three hours with Mrs. Schley, the fortune teller who'd convinced her that the future was not only knowable but could be mastered. Ida's words, after the latest customer departed, were harsh.

"Such darned foolishness, Livy," she said.

"Now, Mother. Don't start with me."

"Wily old crab is taking your money."

"She knows about things, that's all I'll say."

"Throwing hard-earned money down a dry well."

Ida talked like that because she'd lived on a farm with Livy's father until he had a stroke and died in 1942. They were married forty years and she couldn't understand why Livy hadn't settled down. My dad, whom Livy ran off with, had been a rolling stone; my first step dad was a man who treated her bad. Harmon was an ex-high school beau who'd been married before, but they felt getting together was fate. Mrs. Schley advised Livy all would be well, but not without travail. *Travail* was the word Livy emphasized.

"Didn't Mrs. Schley tell me about your attack?" Livy told Ida.

"What in heaven's name are you talking about?"

"When your appendix burst and you nearly died?"

"How could that foolish woman know about that?"

"Well, she did," Livy said. "I had a dream and went to her. She said a loved one was sick but would live. Knowing your disdain for doctors, I phoned and she was right."

"You're so gullible, Livy. She guessed from things you told her before."

"I never did. You think illness is in the mind, but saw a doctor quick enough."

"I fainted dead away and had nothing to do with that."

"Mrs. Schley also said Robby would be in uniform in two years," Livy added. "That worries me, even if it's going to work out okay."

I perked up then, recalling when Livy went to see Mrs. Schley as I sat thinking the woman looked like a witch with a wrinkled face, fingers so long and bony they appeared skinless, and eyes dark as agates. She didn't have a crystal ball, instead a glass pyramid, and bracelets that jangled like tambourines muffled by her red velvet sleeves. When we left, she ran her fingers through my hair, giving me goose bumps because her touch was cold. She made me feel as if wet lint clung to my skin even though she looked as dry as the knit shawls draped over her ornate furnishings.

"Mom, you never told me that," I muttered, breaking into their argument.

"Darned foolishness," Ida said as a customer entered and shopped with a basket hooked over one arm. "Let's hear no more of it."

"It's bound to come true for sure," Livy shot back. "Wait and see."

"Mom," I said, keeping my voice down. "Most guys my age could be in uniform when eighteen because of the draft law passed last year."

Livy gazed at Ida. "There, you see. Mrs. Schley was right after all."

"Where's Harmon?" I said, exasperated with her stubbornness.

"Probably sleeping it off." She smoked a cigarette as Ida waited on the customer. Livy arched her head toward the rear door. "Robby, see if he's up."

"Huh uh." Going to check on him was the last thing I wanted.

"You go on now, just peek in the bedroom for a look-see."

Ida removed her apron, handed it to Livy, and said she'd go herself because she had to use the bathroom. She added that if Harmon was awake she'd give him a piece of her mind. Livy glared at Ida, crushed her cigarette into the ashtray as if squashing a bug, flung the apron across the counter and stomped out, banging the back door. Ida retied the apron, smiling a tight-lipped smile as she winked at me. She waited on an old lady more wizened than her before turning to me with her large hands on her hips.

Standing like that, big-boned, fierce-looking, it was easy to remember that she'd endured a hard-scrabble farm in Minnesota, cooking three meals a day in harvest season, baking bread, churning butter, and whiling away bleak winter months quilting or sewing as blizzard gales screeched. Our time together seemed like episodes from another life.

"I don't mean to speak ill of your mother," Ida said, "but sometimes she acts plain foolish, like a body that hasn't learned anything at all."

"She means well," I said, not trying to defend Livy, but thinking it was true while adding, "good hearted, too. She knows Harmon's upset about this poor grocery store."

"It was Pops," Ida said, referring to my grandfather. "Spoiled her rotten, gave her such high hopes about everything."

I only nodded, having heard that complaint about Livy's defective character and agreeing that it must certainly be true.

"I hope she don't lose her spirit," Ida said, hushing as a man came in, a Mexican who looked like he might be working yards in the neighborhood. She nodded at him, not comfortable around the Mexicans and Negroes who entered. He bought wieners and root beer and left. She turned to me. "About all Livy's got is hope things will get better."

I was hungry and thought about going to the house for a sandwich. The possibility that Livy and Harmon might be talking about things put me off. I went to the bakery rack for a wax-wrapped mini apple pie and gobbled it down. Then I drank a Nehi orange soda. Livy came to relieve Ida at the counter. She tied the dishtowel about her waist. Ida didn't want to leave till Livy pointed toward the back door.

"Oh, go on," she said, "both of you."

Ida said, "Is that darned rascal up?"

"Yes, but he drove away again."

Ida asked, "What did he say?"

"Nothing. Go have lunch."

I followed Ida into the bungalow. Despite my snack in the store, she fixed me a bologna sandwich. She ate cottage cheese and pineapple chunks and was quiet, pausing to shake her head and gaze right through me. Ida was a handsome woman with creamy, wrinkled skin and bright green eyes. In a way we were closer than I was with Livy because I'd been packed off to Ida between Mom's marriages.

"There's been trouble like this before," I said.
Ida sighed. "I reckon that's true enough."
"What'll we do if they split up again?"
"Again?" she said. "Harmon and Livy?"
"Yeah, Last year, for two or three weeks."
"I didn't know. Well, if it's to be…."
"What'll happen to you and me?"
"I expect we'll go on, like before."

She was referring to the times Livy had parked me on the farm. I had moved so much and been in so many schools that they were a blur. Not belonging any one place haunted me at night before sleep--it was on my mind Saturday night listening to them fighting. It was a duet of anger from earliest memories: Livy and my dad, Livy and Mr. Brogan, and now Livy and Harmon. I hoped there'd be an end to it, but never believed. Ida reached across the table to pat my arm.

"You worry way too much, Robby."
"I can't seem to help myself."
"Just put things out of mind."
"How am I supposed to do that?"

Before she could answer, the Plymouth pulled into the dirt drive beside the store. Harmon got out, opened the trunk lid, and carted produce boxes inside. It seemed that I should go help, but I didn't. Instead, I sat and watched until he had unloaded five boxes and stayed in the store. Ida cleared the table, rinsed dishes in the sink, sipped a glass of tap water, and then went to her room for a rest. I watched out the front window a while, then returned to the store. Harmon unpacked lettuce, trimmed wilted edges and stacked the heads in a pyramid. He'd already dealt with the celery, carrots, green onions and radishes.

Livy was at the counter dealing with customers. I helped Harmon with oranges, apples, melons and bananas. He didn't look at me as he worked. His face was red, and he'd nicked himself shaving, which left a cut on his left cheek red with dried blood. His eyes were bleary, neck skin slack, and he seemed indolent, unfocused. But he'd done this work so often that the fruit and vegetables were neatly arranged.

As I toted the wood boxes to the back room, someone requested a trimmed roast. That required Harmon to open the meat case and do some cutting with a butcher knife. I got back while he and Livy were chatting as if nothing unpleasant had happened. It was almost three. I asked if there was more to do. They stared as if I'd suddenly come upon them. It made me feel strange, and they grunted that it was okay to leave. I hurried to the bungalow. It was still too early to head for Mrs. Bender's restaurant, but I wanted to get away. I changed to denims and a clean T-shirt.

Ida lay stretched on her bed, shades drawn half way. She had removed her shoes, the large feet crossed in white ankle socks. I thought she was asleep, but her eyes opened. Lying down she seemed smaller, maybe because the iron bedstead was so huge. Her lips moved but no words came out. I eased into the room to see if she wanted something. She gazed at me before asking what was going on in our small region of the universe.

"Where...?" she uttered in a mushy way as I sensed she'd removed her false teeth and they were soaking in the glass on the nightstand. "What are you doing?"

"I'm leaving soon to work at Mrs. Bender's restaurant."

She shook her head. "Where Livy and...Harmon?"

"In the store, Ida. Working together."

"Uh huh." Ida studied me. "You all right?"

"I'm okay." She watched, curious. "They're okay, too."

"Surely." She was either half asleep or just patient about everything except Livy's foolishness. "Where're you off to?"

"My job at Mrs. Bender's. You know, dish washing and helping out."

"Your job." Her eyes were wide open now. "You going to be all right?"

"Yeah." But I wasn't sure. The move to Ojai, I thought we were settling down at last. It was too much to hope for. Other kids led ordinary lives with normal mothers and fathers while I lived with constant turmoil and anxiety. "I'd better get going."

"You'll be fine," she said, reaching for me. I went to her. She clenched her hands around mine so tight I felt she wouldn't ever let go. "You're strong, Robby. Standing up to many trials. Remarkable and amazing."

"What do you mean?" No one had ever talked to me like that.

"Remember on the farm?" she said, taking deep breaths to not only recollect a time long ago but also get it out in one burst. "Helping with chores, going down the hill to the school bus in such bitter cold you were numb. Thunder and lighting stormy nights?"

"Yeah, that was sure a long while back."

"It was rough on you," Ida said. "I never told you what a comfort it was to have you with us--me and Pops. After his stroke and he couldn't work the place, it would've been awful if not for your wild boyishness to keep us going."

I figured being farmed out to them was a burden, and it would have been better if they didn't have me to care for. I thought about Livy and Harmon attempting to make life work, and Ida before me, breathing deep, smiling. She was talking about the long winters, and how I played beneath the quilt frame as she cut and pieced remnants into a fabric mosaic that stretched above with a kerosene lamp emblazoning the multi-colored patches. She pretended to not know what odd-shaped piece came next and begged me to study the pattern and help her decide. I crouched below, sorting myriad pieces of cotton, no two alike, puzzled about how anything useful could ever come from such confusion.

It was a kaleidoscope of stripes, polka dots, flowers, checks, gingham and pastels in red, yellow, blue, green, orange, purple and colors that resonated like poetry when she said them--magenta, lavender and lapis lazuli. I recalled Ida's lilting voice: *Bringing In The Sheaves* and *Blest Be The Tie That Binds,* and remembered her stitching castoffs into a glorious coverlet. Now, she kept talking as her voice fell to a whisper. I waited until she was fast asleep before I departed for another job and devoted myself to blessed busyness.

SLOUCH

~~~

Okay, Gos was blubbery. But that's no reason to torture him. The worst thing about gym class first thing each morning was that it messed up the whole day. Get to Burbank High at eight to go to the sweat-stink locker room and put on swim trunks? But that's the way it went, topped off by Mr. Bildruff, the bald tyrant of the teaching staff. He taught Social Studies in the bullish manner he displayed around the swim pool--it wouldn't have shocked me to see him blow that damned whistle of his during pop quizzes. Gos was Mort Gosberger, a dough-faced kid not only huge for sixteen at two hundred pounds, but also sluggish, good-natured, slow to anger, and the target of practical jokes.

He wasn't dumb, but had a naturally lethargic manner due to his size and years of being singled out for ridicule. After warm up, Mr. Bildruff, 'Baldy Bildy' behind his back, emitted a red-faced blast on his whistle. That ordered us goose-pimpled slaves to plunge into the water. There's no civil description of a high school swimming pool; the closest was the 'aaagh!' from twenty-five freezing boys subjecting their adolescent bodies to its chlorine frigidity. The toxic perfumery lingered on shriveled skin the rest of the day, and the sting around the eyes meant tears without emotion.

But the worst part was the total physical exhaustion of gasping and gulping swim laps. It was all I could do to go the distance as Baldy Bildy shrilled the whistle and shouted at laggards. The most abused was Gos, who one would expect might slip through the water like a greased whale, but actually floundered and flailed with no forward momentum. He did only than two laps. Baldy Bildy hovered above Gos calling out 'slob' and 'fatso' without urging the kid to further effort and, while the rest of us showered, kept him in the pool as punishment. Although we kidded Gos, it was hard not to feel sorry for him. What could we do, worn out and hustling toward our next class?

That was the routine three mornings a week during the fall semester. I stopped paying attention to Gos and didn't realize the kid was making progress. He got to the point where he did six of the required ten laps. His torso acquired muscle, so much that Baldy Bildy badgered him about going out for football or the wrestling team. Gos grinned and shrugged. The idea that he might engage in any activity that involved aggression seemed foreign, and the topic, but not the teasing, was dropped. In Baldy Bildy's Social Studies class, Gos would be addressed when he got a 'B' or an 'A' on a quiz and goaded to put those smarts to good use on the football team playing all three linemen on the right or left side. That brought guffaws from the students.

It was by chance that I discovered Gos one Friday afternoon engaged in exercises in the gymnasium. I'd gone to the locker to get my raunchy swimsuit to take home. Gos was weight training, clutching, hoisting, and pressing one huge barbell. His face was flushed, eyes tight. After watching him a while I turned to leave, figuring he had decided to join the

HUNCHING HOMEWARD

football or wrestling team. He grunted my name, gave me his slow smile, and continued. I saw him other times running the varnished boards around the gym in a stolid way as if chasing nothing but still determined to get somewhere.

The peculiar thing was, the more Gos improved, the greater the goading aroused in Baldy Bildy. During agonizing morning swims, which I dreaded all day Sunday since I'd be weary on Mondays, Wednesdays and Fridays, any hope I had of enjoying school vanished. But Gos was able to complete nine laps. Rather than encourage him to greater accomplishment, Baldy Bildy increased taunting him as the rest of us, along the side of the pool with our feet dangling in the tepid water, sat hunched over, embarrassed for Gos. Into the tenth lap, he began to flail until, nearly sinking. Baldy Bildy started blowing that damned whistle, groused about slouching and gutlessness, and waved Gos in.

Two weeks before the semester ended, in a repetition of the dreary routine, when Baldy Bildy hesitated to blow his whistle as Gos struggled lamely to complete half of the final lap, it was clear to us watchers that he was trying to bully the kid to go all the way. Gos flapped like a creature in its death throes, beating the water with his massive arms but not moving ahead. He sank deeper till his head went under. Baldy Bildy stood waiting, whistle in his mouth, while the curious class perked up. We felt something ominous was happening. I stood, shivering while my toes curled at the edge of the concrete. Others ranged alongside, watching Gos sink down to the blue pool bottom.

I was unable to breathe without forcing myself, as though readying for the rescue effort I sensed approaching. How many of us would have to dive deep and struggle to lift the enormous boy who only wanted to succeed at his greatest challenge? Before anyone moved, Gos crouched underwater and propeled upward using his legs. He broke the surface like a breaching leviathan, flapped his arms, and with a lunge, reached for the side of the pool. He was close enough for us, extending our hands, to pull him to safety, choking and spitting.

Baldy Bildy shouted, 'Nice going, slouch. You got another ten feet--all the way to the bottom of the pool!'

Gos missed school for a week and returned with a note that kept him out of the pool. He sat clothed on a wood bench while the rest of us did our agonizing laps. It was clear that he'd get no grade if he didn't complete the required ten laps sometime. Baldy Bildy whistled and yelled at the rest of us Monday and Wednesday morning, and continued calling Gos 'slouch.'

On Friday, Gos came out in his swimsuit and, without a word, swam. He was slow, but kept going, lap after lap, until the ninth when he appeared played out but kept stroking. Baldy Bildy paced the edge, silent, eyes cold. We sat watching, hoping. Finally, Gos struggled to the end of the tenth lap. We rushed to help him out. We were slapping him on the back when Baldy Bildy arrived, both beefy hands on his hips. He shook his domed head in gruff disbelief. Before he could turn away and blow his whistle, ending the class, Gos, still flushed and breathless from his incredible effort, grabbed him in a bear hug, carried him to the edge of the pool deck as he muttered 'Baldy Bildy, Baldy Bildy', hoisted him like a pliable barbell, and hurled him out into the water. More a splat than a splash. The man surfaced spitting and spluttering.

The class laughed and ran for the showers. We piled up to crowd through the door and were almost inside when we heard the whistle blow. It wasn't the usual harsh screech that raised goose bumps but, instead, a gurgly wail. Gos, and those of us close to the pool, looked around to see Baldy Bildy flailing like a helpless child. There is no explaining our inertia except the shock of discovering that the nemesis of our suffering couldn't swim! We hurried back, not sure what to do as the dreaded authority figure sank under.

I'd like to relate that we all leapt in to pull him out, but we didn't. It was Gos who hit the water with a colossal splurge, went straight to the bottom, grabbed Baldy Bildy, and walked him underwater to the shallow end and safety. Gos kneeled over him to press the water out until the man coughed and sat up. Gos didn't get thanked for the rescue since he'd thrown him into the pool, but he passed the course right enough.

THE GUY SHE CHOSE

W eird things happen to you when young that you'd like to forget but just keep coming back to screw up your life. What pisses me off is the way Loretta Blythe sticks in my mind like sludge. It happened so long ago that no way could I even be the same guy I was then. I mean, high school, for god's sakes. She was not only beautiful in a 1951 kind of way--checked pleated skirts cut just above the knees, white cotton blouses that couldn't disguise the full rapture of her bosom, an oval face with thick lips like a movie star cosmetics advertisement, and red honey blonde hair parted in the middle with tumbling curls down the back and over each ear. She wasn't Lana Turner, but for Glendale High she was superb. She was so cool that any hope of getting on her dance card was nonexistent.

Since it was clear to me as a lowly Junior as she cut a social swath through the Senior class that year hanging on the arm of Jerry Hackett, the football quarterback, that I would have a better chance of dating Marilyn Monroe or Debbie Reynolds, I contented myself with what now might be called a 'stealth' approach. Whenever I caught sight of her coming my way in the hall between classes, especially when she was accompanied by fewer than two or three of her girl cohorts, I would smile and say something cheery like, 'Hi there, Loretta!' or 'You're lookin' great, Loretta'. She didn't know who I was and nodded without breaking stride or conversation. But I knew her travel path and always found a way to perform my ritual greeting.

To appreciate the challenge, you have to know that I was medium height, not athletic--I managed to survive P. E. where we wore blue cotton shorts and T shirts to run around the track until exhausted or played witless basketball on the asphalt paved courts--while the guys around Loretta poised to leap if Jerry Hackett faltered were husky beyond Tarzan of the Apes and also more than handsome. I was barely average, but considered my face pleasantly arranged, and Mom drooled over my blue eyes and opulent lashes. She also said my smile was sincere.

For weeks, overcome with guilt pangs and frustration due to lack of response, I gave Loretta my daily routine. Monday through Friday I endured amused stares from Loretta's hangers-on. But one day, she glanced my way with a radiant smile. I imagined she'd said 'Hi', but I didn't hear anything because the shock numbed my hearing. No guy ever entranced by a princess far beyond his realm can grasp the anguish of such striving. I won't say my grades suffered, because I was at most a 'B' student with occasional flashes of 'A-Minus'. But I soon realized there wouldn't be any 'A' that semester because of gross infatuation. My morale surged during lunch hour one day when I skimmed through the cafeteria with my tray toward the table by the corner window. Loretta was there all by herself! I looked around in panic to see if she'd simply gotten there ahead of her friends, but nobody came. I was paralyzed with both fright and possibility, and could only stand in front of her without speaking or moving.

She looked up before forking salad into her mouth. "Hi, there."

"Oh, sure," I muttered with the aplomb of a fool. "How're you?"

"Aw right," she said, chewing while she teased flaming tresses.

"That's good." I tried to steady myself as I put my dishes down.

"Do I know ya?" she said after I sat across from her.

I played it bold. "I'm Burk. See you lots in the hall."

"Oh, yeah, sure." She blinked a couple times. "Burk?"

"Yeah, Burk Rodgers."

She laughed. "Like Buck Rogers?"

God, I made her laugh! "Sure, with a 'D'."

"Oh, yeah," she said, but she didn't get it. "We have classes together?"

"No, but I see you around school a lot."

"Yeah, that figures 'cause I'm kinda popular."

While we ate I kept looking around, waiting for some of her girl buddies to show up, but none did. In her serene presence I found myself with nothing to say. Everything I'd rehearsed before this moment, the neat ideas I'd figured on chatting up to impress her, drained from my head like water from a rusty bucket. I tried not to stare as she ate while giving me occasional glances. She wore jangly bracelets on both wrists, and had an elegant-looking watch. Her pink sweater was fluffy like a cat and knocked me over with a bosom that would've done a starlet proud. As I said, I didn't want to stare, but I must have without knowing because she looked at me with eyes pinched tight and her lips straight.

"What's the matta?' she said, stern-like, staring me down.

I had to struggle for breath. "Nothing's the matter."

"Why ya lookin' at me like that for?"

"Like what?" My hands were sweaty.

"Like ya was jus' doin'."

"I wasn't," but my denial lacked believability.

She smiled without teeth. "Well, don' do it, okay?"

"I wasn't. But if you think I was, I'm real sorry."

"Well, aw right, then." She smiled half way pretty, nice teeth, and kept eating.

"Besides," I said, deciding to take another big gamble because faint heart never won fair lady, or some such crap, "it's hard not to admire you."

"Oh?" she said, and even stopped forking cake.

"Can't help myself." That was the godawful truth.

She smiled big now. "Yeah?"

"Like I said, Loretta, I've seen you lots, and like looking at you."

"No kiddin'?" She finished her cake, leaving a smudge of chocolate frosting in the left corner of her mouth. "Why's that, anyway?"

"I just do," I said, wanting to reach over and flick that morsel onto a finger so I could lick it. "You're like a movie star, the way you walk around."

"No kiddin'!" she said with a laugh. I was really getting to her.

"Sure. I wouldn't say something like that if I didn't really mean--"

"Hey, Loretta!" It was Jerry Hackett, striding over to the table in jeans.

She glared when she saw him, while I slumped to make myself smaller. The spaghetti on my plate now had the appeal of leftovers.

"Where ya been?' she said to him, mad-like. "I almost finished lunch."

"Had things to do, that's where." He looked at me. "Who's this?"

I hesitated to give my right name, but Loretta said, "Buck Rogers."

Hackett smiled, then laughed real hard. "Yeah, I believe that, all right."

"It's my real name," I said, adding, "Rodgers with a 'D'."

He didn't get it any more than Loretta had, and said, "Huh?"

"You coulda told me ya weren't comin'," Loretta said, still upset.

"Yeah," he said, keeping his eyes on me. "Like I told you."

She said, "I don't think I want to talk to ya right now."

"That's okay with me," he said, examining me like I was a bug.

"Well, okay then," Loretta said, and gave me a quick flashing smile as if it was time to get back to the important stuff we'd been discussing. She ignored Hackett as he gave a shrug before sauntering away. She watched him go and then looked at me. "He thinks he's so swell. Does jus' what he wants. Well, I don't like it one bit."

"He shouldn't treat you like that." I was taking her side because it seemed the only way to advance my own cause. "You deserve better."

"Thas right," she said. She studied me pensively, then Hackett, who'd stopped on his way out of the cafeteria to chat it up with his gargantuan buddies. While she examined me she had a sneaky, secret face. "Ya goin' to the dance Friday night?"

It was so sudden my heart seemed to stop, my breathing, too. My first response came out a complete lie since I'd never imagined attending. "Thought I might."

"Got a date?" The way she said it, perfectly honest question.

"Not at this time," I managed. Not any time, truth to tell.

"Maybe I'll see ya there--okay?"

"Sure, why not?" I wanted to talk more, linger in her company, but she stood up with her tray and started to leave. "I'll look for you at the dance, Loretta."

"Swell." She sauntered away. "Ya be sure and do that, Buck Rogers."

I don't have to tell you that for the rest of the school week I was a physical and emotional wreck. My intentional encounters with Loretta in the halls were intense because she smiled and waved, and also stopped to chat, making a point of telling her girl friends my name. It was all I could do to keep from making an idiot of myself in front of them, but they didn't pay me any special notice so I didn't have to put on an act. By Friday night I was so nervous I didn't think I could attend the dance without getting sick. I donned my blue serge suit with a tie from Dad's closet, and went. I noticed Loretta in a green satin dress that flared away like a hoop-skirted Southern belle.

A combo of guitar, saxophone, clarinet, trumpet, trombone, piano and drums from the junior college already droned *Harbor Lights*, but nobody was on the dance floor yet. The girls and guys were sort of lined up across the gymnasium from one another, except for a few couples that had come together, and clusters of guys and girls huddled talking and looking miserable. As Hackett entered with three of his buddies, I sidled away. I don't know if Loretta saw him or not, but just after the band started *Goodnight Irene* and a few couples eased out to start dancing, she came striding directly across the floor leading three of her friends. Before I could say anything, she clasped my hand and led me onto the dance floor. The girls, giggling and laughing, latched onto other boys at the same time, none of them, I realized, from the athletic crowd.

Suddenly there we were, a bunch of us guys who, if we went to the dances at all, usually ended up standing around the gym wall most of the night watching everyone else have a good time. I wasn't just embracing Loretta Blythe, The Magnificent, but actually whirling about with her left hand on my shoulder and her strong right clasping my left hand so tight that I don't think I could have pulled away if I wanted to. I didn't hear the music, and my most active sensation was seeing the rest of the swirling dancers, and the entire room with its overhead lights turned down, through the floating blonde strands of her hair--overcome with a scent that I would later learn was Jean Nate perfume. It obliterated the hoped-for power of my Aqua Velva lotion I'd splashed on without shaving.

I tried to act cool and calm, but Loretta and her girls were so in charge of me and all the fortunate wallflowers they'd swept into their cotillion, that it was easier to let everything happen. When one song ended and another began, Loretta would pass me to one of her giggling friends and take another of the group they'd corralled as their partners. This went on until a fourth tune started and Loretta was back with me. I wasn't smart enough to mind or get tired, switching from blonde Loretta to brown-haired Patsy, then a red head called Sylvia, then a black-haired girl with peach-colored skin who was Anna Lucia--I think.

When the band took an intermission and we gathered as four couples near the punch bowl and cookies, I noticed Hackett and some of his buddies lingering nearby. I excused myself and went to the men's room. Since I didn't know the other three guys who had been recruited as part of the quartet of dancing fools, it felt good to get off by myself for a few minutes. Unfortunately, the break didn't last long. As I unzipped at a urinal, Hackett came alongside to pee, as did one of his buddies on the other side of me. I almost couldn't do my own business, but did squeeze out a few drops and zip up. At the washbasin, Hackett rinsed his hands and stared at me in the mirror. I did my best to ignore him, but it was impossible.

"What the hell you think you're doing?" he said with a big teeth smile.

"I'm not doing anything," I said, my legs wobbly from dancing so much.

"Think you're pretty damned cute out there, don't you?"

"No," I said, not feeling cute at all right then. "I don't."

"She rubbing up against you a lot, kid?"

"What the--no!"

"Maybe," said the other guy Hackett had come in with, who had the basin on the other side of me, "he thinks he's going to cut your time, Jer."

"No!" I said, looking around quick for a paper towel.

"Just forget about it, see?" Hackett told me.

They dried their hands with towels while I watched, letting water drip from my fingers onto the cement floor. When they left in their dark brown sport coats and tan slacks with soft white turtlenecks, I couldn't help shivering. During this time, other guys came in and out of the men's room without paying more than casual attention to the three of us. It was the loneliest time I'd ever known--being amid so many guys who not only didn't care about what was happening but avoiding involvement. It was a brutal realization that a single person could be threatened or attacked without any prospect of sympathy or help from fellow human beings.

I remained in the men's room for several more minutes, sweating and cold, washed my hands and face again with tap water, and stalled dabbing myself with a paper towel. When I couldn't put it off any longer, I returned to the gym. Loretta and her group still clung with the hapless dance partners who looked dazed by their good fortune. She put a hand on my shoulder while holding a punch cup in the other. She smiled, but in a detached manner, as if something sober darkened her mood.

"Ya were gone a long time, Bucky," she said.

"Yeah, it was crowded in there."

"I saw big shot Jerry. He say anythin'?"

"Jerry?" I was tempted, but didn't. "No."

"He didn't say nothin'?" She sounded disappointed, and gazed across the room to where Hackett and his buddies were talking and laughing it up with a gaggle of girls. "Nothin' at all?"

The combo kicked in with *Tennessee Waltz*.

"That's awful strange," she said with a far off look.

Before she could say anything more, I clasped her hand and led her back onto the dance floor while she kept staring toward him. She seemed stiff in my arms, so I tried to move more smoothly and turn her around with my basic two-step, the only thing I could accomplish to the beat of the music. My mom wanted to teach me other dance steps, but I never saw a reason for it till now. Loretta still felt beautiful to me and looked as good as before; she was especially warm, and slivers of blonde hair clung to her forehead, temples and neck. When I turned her away from where I recalled Jerry might be standing, she craned her head around. It began to bother me, and I began thinking 'what the hell' and going out of my way to turn her fast, jerking her off balance. She was just about my size, but since I was concentrating and getting a bit peeved, I managed to move her where I wanted even when she resisted a little.

As we danced I lost track of her girl friends until it occurred to me that they were close by but dancing with other guys than the gang of us they had picked up earlier. When I felt the hard tap on my shoulder, I knew who it was before turning. He took Loretta's hand from my shoulder, placing it on his. As she unlaced the fingers of her right hand from my left, a sweaty emptiness lingering in my palm, I knew the evening was over. It had been great while it lasted, but a crushing reality to be reminded that it was not to be--was never meant to be.

"S'long, Bucky," Loretta whispered laughing when he swept her away.

"See ya around, kid," Hackett tossed at me as he twirled past into the crowd.

I didn't have sense enough to get off the dance floor, and stood there like a total moron while couples bounced against me with hips, shoulders and elbows. I didn't mind being used by Loretta, or discarded, because she wasn't as great as I had hoped. What made me bitter was the guy she chose. I wish that it had all happened different. I should have walked away rather than played Loretta's game. I could have, and that would really be worth remembering.

HUNCHING HOMEWARD

I was the only soldier on the bus from Los Angeles to Badersville in March '51. My National Guard unit got activated in September and we were heading overseas for training in Japan before going to Korea. An obligatory visit home to L. A. embroiled me in Mother's failing marriage with a third husband, and then I caught the bus north to visit Donald and Maura. They were both seniors at Badersville High, something I had avoided by going on active duty. We'd goofed off since seventh grade, Donald the studious, shy friend; and Maura, a vivacious girl. Why she liked me I didn't know. My move to L. A. meant writing letters to them, which I did sporadically till I got to camp. Then I wrote weekly. She replied less often, but cordially.

As the bus descended the mountain into the valley with its potato, sugar beet and cotton fields, I breathed deeper. I didn't expect Donald or Maura to be at the station since it was Friday and they'd be at school. My olive drab uniform felt stiff instead of martial. But, it was a banner of maturity; a soldier wasn't a child, rather, someone who has moved into adulthood. At camp I drank beer and smoked even if it irritated my sinuses. I was returning different than the pimply junior of nine months before.

The bus pulled into the station. I stood with my canvas pass bag in a hurry to get off. I'd never been in that part of Badersville with bars and fleabag hotels that catered to winos, farm laborers and oil field workers. A few Mexicans and old folks acted confused as they left the bus to stand on the sidewalk beside their suitcases. I put on my overseas cap and sauntered to Main Street, at ease amid people who gave me respectful looks. I acted like one of those soldiers from World War II, warriors with ribbons and rank.

Away from downtown crowds, heading for Donald's house past dry lawns shaded by oaks, elms and pines, I swelled with pride being back in the place I'd lived longest-- five years--after a rootless childhood. Suddenly, I was elated, more full of life than ever before. Just the idea of sharing my status as an adult with high school friends, adventures I knew would amaze them, filled me with happiness. My heart surged as if running the combat course with live machine gun fire. I controlled my excitement when I saw the single-story stucco house with oleanders. I knew Donald would be home because I had phoned before catching the bus.

He opened the door and smiled, glad to see me. He led me to the kitchen where he was having a bologna sandwich and glass of milk. While fixing me the same, I noted that he was taller by two inches and had filled out like his dad, a railroad fireman. His mom was a nurse at Perce County General Hospital and would come home soon. We chatted while eating but soon became quiet. He wore his curly brown hair long, his face still thin and quizzical like the much better student than I ever was.

I waited for him to ask about the army. Instead, he wanted to know how long I'd stay. Sunday I had to grab a bus west back to camp. I realized he didn't know what to do with me for the weekend. I meant to spend time with him but also Maura. I asked about her. He shrugged and said she was fine. Did he talk to her often? *Only now and then.* Had he told her I was coming for a visit? *Yes.* Did he think she was home? *Probably.* Would it be okay to phone her? *Yeah, sure.* I dialed. It rang seven times till she answered. 'Hi' was all I managed. 'You've arrived,' she said, her voice steady as I pictured her honey-blond curls and upturned nose. If there was more to say, it was up to me since she was silent.

How was she? *Fine.* Would she have time to get together tonight? She wasn't sure since she didn't know what the family was doing. That crushed my ebullience, which fell more when she said she might have to see her grandparents. I pressed for a date till she agreed to a movie Saturday night. I hung up. Donald paged a *Popular Mechanics* as I got back to the kitchen. I told him Maura couldn't go out till the next night. I asked about his plans after graduation. He had a chemistry scholarship to Stanford. His life appeared stable and mine seemed unfocused. It made me queasy. I went to wash in the bathroom, staring at my pink face and smooth cheeks. I only shaved every three days. What had I expected after almost a year? I'd been away longer than I had lived most places.

But I brightened when Donald's mom, Tillie, got in. She hugged me in such a heartfelt way that I was startled. One reason I'd hung around Donald was that Tillie often treated me more lovingly than my mother, as if she understood my life better than I did. She looked matronly in her white uniform, bracing me at arm's length to fuss over my snazzy appearance. 'My, oh my,' was all she said as she clasped me again, my face into soft brown hair smelling of an astringent that suggested mortality. She rushed to change clothes and returned in jeans and sweatshirt.

'What were our plans for the evening?' she asked. Donald shrugged, leaving me to reply as Tillie bustled around the kitchen. I explained about getting together with Maura on Saturday night. After a glance at Donald, Tillie said that would be nice and Donald should ask Caroline, a neighbor, and it'd be nice for a double date. We could use the car, her '47 Studebaker. She urged Donald to phone the girl, and when he came back into the kitchen he told us Caroline could go. I phoned Maura to explain and she sounded okay with it.

During a meal of left over meatloaf, Tillie said she'd fix something special on Sunday. For a couple hours we sat in the living room, chatting about school, family, and army life. We turned on the television with its tiny oval screen enlarged by a plastic magnifier and watched a Hoot Gibson western. I got tired the longer I sat in the lounge chair, and excused myself. I went to bed, only stirring once when Donald's dad, Ardry, came in from his freight route at three a.m. In the morning I awoke after nine, numb, more than tired. I felt hollow, as if this awkward visit was turning into a waste of time. It might've been better to return to camp early, or get a room in San Luis Obispo to wander on my own. But after washing up and joining Tillie and Donald in the kitchen, things brightened. We had a huge breakfast of bacon, eggs, hotcakes and coffee. Donald was talkative. His dad came in and was pleased to see me, and I felt much better.

Ardry, a nickname for Willard, drove us to a pool hall at noon where we spent three hours playing and slinging the bull. He wanted to know about my training, compared it to his navy time, and with the winking complicity of the owner, saw to it that Donald and I drank a couple beers. We smoked the strong cigars he'd passed to each of us. When we left, Ardry felt great, having put away several beers and bourbon shots. Donald drove us home while Ardry talked railroading, fishing, hunting, and damned Truman getting us into Korea. Later I called Maura to confirm our movie date.

After munching sandwiches, showering, and cleaning up, Donald went over to pick up Caroline. He came back with a slight girl--thin, red-brown hair, a wan smile that made her gray eyes crinkle. Her voice was so deeply sultry it made me smile since she appeared younger than eighteen in her pleated plaid skirt, orange blouse, beige sweater and saddle shoes, more like a junior high school girl. We drove in the gray Studebaker across town to Maura's on a hillside above the spangle of Badersville's lights. It was a dry, chill night and clear sky with a swatch of stars. I'd seen such nights before, but at that moment it felt precious, something I might not see again and therefore something to secure in memory. Maura came out the door. I'd forgotten how pretty she was, or maybe she'd become prettier. Much as I wanted to act older, more mature than these people I'd left behind, Maura was the one who'd grown into a young woman.

Sitting in front with Donald during the drive into downtown, Caroline made small talk with Maura, but was soon quieted into silence as we listened to the engine and stared at passing sights. The movie was about Marines fighting on a Jap island in World War II. It made me more self-conscious in my uniform, sitting in the dark next to Maura, Caroline and Donald watching Richard Widmark in *Halls of Montezuma*. When it ended, we drifted out with the Saturday night throng. Maura suggested a hamburger diner.

In the back seat, having said nothing personal since I'd picked her up, I reached for her right hand to hold as we had done often before. She let me, but I sensed it wasn't something she wanted, and after a bit I let go. She wasn't unfriendly, just polite. I was glad when we got to the diner and sat in a booth. The routine of ordering took several minutes, during which I glanced at Maura as Caroline talked about school. I got the oddest feeling that Donald and Caroline were cordial at the same time he and Maura seemed distracted and distant.

While waiting for our food, I kept asking myself who these people were. Caroline was more friendly after only casual acquaintance than Donald or Maura. Had we changed so much in less than a year that we had little in common except an early adolescent friendship? Everyone got chatty when food came, hamburgers, fries and malted milks lubricating conversation. I described army life, amusing them with gas training when I had to remove my mask before leaving the tent and got tongue-tied as I tried to say name, rank and serial number to an officer.

We lingered after eating but finally admitted we couldn't avoid the waitress who wanted to seat fresh patrons in the booth. Although my Private's pay was meager by civilian standards, it gave me the chance to pick up the check and assume a larger adult status than these high school companions. But walking to the car, I sensed that my visit was a futile effort to return to a time better left behind. I was disappointed with Maura, having sneaked looks while she ate and also eyed Donald, who used to be cheerful rather than somber. They remained aloof, as if isolated from Caroline and myself.

On the drive to Maura's house, I held her hand once again and tried to talk about seeing her Sunday. She was noncommittal, and I gave up. At her door, holding her hand, I made a last effort to save the night as I leaned close to kiss her. She shifted so my lips brushed her cheek. She said it was *nice* to see me again, and she'd had a *nice* time.

I was angrily walking to the car before I heard her front door close behind me. On the drive to Donald and Caroline's, they talked as I sulked. They asked me a question about when was I shipping out, where was I going in Japan, would I be going to Korea? I replied the best I could. Donald stopped the car at Caroline's house and walked her to the door, and then drove a block farther on and parked in his driveway. When we got out, I took a moment to examine the sky and stars again. I longed to reach the specks of light so far beyond my pitiful life.

That night I tossed, unable to sleep, trying to grasp what was wrong, why I didn't belong anywhere or to anybody. Sunday dinner was roast chicken, corn on the cob, mashed potatoes, and apple pie. Ardry ate more than the rest of us combined. I tried to phone Maura. No answer. I asked Donald why she seemed so strange. He thought it was because I'd been gone too long. He drove me to the station. We shook hands, and as he drove off it came to me that I would never see him again. I verified my ticket and waited on a wood bench with two soldiers, gaunt aliens like myself. Before departure I phoned Maura again; her dad said she was out.

Three months later she sent me a short letter in Japan. She was engaged to Donald. I got busy preparing for Korea, thinking *now* rather than *yesterday* or *tomorrow*, no longer dwelling on where I belonged. Simple every day existence had become a timely home unto itself.

THE HALLELUJAH KID

It is my firm conviction that I was destined to be irreligious. First, because my much-married- and-divorced mother insisted I should have religion in my life to offset youthful chaos; second, I was sent to unorthodox churches. In my early life, it was a preacher's world. When I came upon Buddhism, Confucianism, Hinduism, Islam, Taoism, Zoroastrianism, Druidism, and the Greco Roman gods, I was already full of Evangelical, Pentecostal and Revival Christianity.

That I avoided fanaticism is due to a twist of fate and act of supreme devilishness. In the beginning (note the Biblical effect), Mom was influenced by Grandma Ida's Christian Science. Images of Ida sitting in a rocker reading *Science and Health With Key To the Scriptures* by Mary Baker Eddy linger in memory. For a long time I thought the religion was founded by somebody named 'Eddie' who was a friend of Jesus. It had to do with God being good, and illness being evil and false belief; if you got sick it was error because you didn't believe strong enough. When I had German measles, Mom got the doctor as Grandma fretted. When Grandpa had one of his heart attacks, Ida prayed and consulted a Christian Science Practitioner. Looking back, it occurs to me that I made an early distinction between body and soul before knowing which one needed the most attention. As a child and totally primitive creature, I gravitated to physicality rather than spirituality due to constant hunger and toilet activity. But I worried about suffering for violating invisible rules of an awesome power hovering beyond human sight.

I was weaned on severe Protestantism by whatever church happened to be closest. While Mom and I stayed with elderly couples in their houses or we rented apartments between frequent stays in drab hotels, she managed to find a nearby Sunday school for me. Never did she attend, saying she'd already acquired all the spirituality and godliness she wanted. Thus I was washed in a sea of religiosity at an age of innocent acceptance and absorbed multiple impressions of faith and belief that molded, or warped, my character.

Since I liked my mother and thought we were living a life of adventure, meeting new people and moving on before we got bored, I embraced each of these new churches on their own merits. At first she was satisfied that I was getting what I needed to become a decent person. I learned how God created the world with Adam and Eve and their fall in the Garden of Eden, but it didn't bother me when they got kicked out because they would surely have gotten tired of it anyway. Thinking back, there was a remarkable consistency between the Biblical teachings of the sects. Sunday school snacks varied from bread and jam, to crackers, cookies, and leaden donuts baked by church ladies thin as scarecrows.

When I lived with Aunt Coletta, the sister of one of Mom's early husbands, I attended a number of camp meetings and revivals during hot humid summer days and nights on the Dakota prairie. They were different from most of the Sunday schools I'd attended. For one thing, they were noisier, with men, women and kids sitting on wood benches as they clapped their hands, stomped their feet, and sang with such gusto God surely heard us no matter how far away He might be.

There was talk about what would happen to pitiful mortals if we somehow didn't obey the Commandments and live more holy lives. I will only mention in retrospect that the wild-eyed, flailing-hair, thunderous voices of the preachers were powerful enough to convince me the fires of Hell must be a hundred times hotter than any day I'd yet lived. As they called the faithful up to be saved and deposit a donation to support the work of the Lord, I went a half dozen times. Aunt Coletta believed I was in dire need of salvation, and she must have considered each quarter she gave me for the offering a sound investment in my holy future.

However, it was disappointing that what I was learning about the Lord didn't have the same effect on many of the adults as it did on me. For example, sin was evil. Yet most of the adults indulged in a variety of sins. Cigars, pipes and cigarettes were condemned, but not always. Strong drink like beer, moonshine and whiskey was wrong, along with a sin called intoxication, which brought on a like-sounding malady, fornication.

The most confusing admonition was to not blaspheme--cussing or taking the name of the Lord in vain. That made me sensitive to proclaimed 'God Almightys' and 'Lordys' which were okay, and 'Goddammits' and 'Goddamneds' which were straight-to-Hell blasphemies. It became clear that men were more prone to sin and the temptations of the devil than women. The worst sins a woman could commit had to do with disobedience, bad housekeeping, gossip, and being taken in adultery, which made even less sense than fornication and intoxication.

What happened was so gradual that it was years before I rebelled. It happened like this. At dinner with Grandma

Ida and Grandpa Lem, I'd announce what would happen to people if they disobeyed the laws of God. For example, it was plain to me that Grandpa's cigars made him liable to end up in Hell, a pure shame because Grandma was certain to go to Heaven even though she sometimes gossiped with neighbor ladies and enjoyed a nip of elderberry wine. They were horrified by my providential judgment and wanted to know how on earth I'd come up with such ideas. When I said the Sunday school lesson inspired such remarks, phone calls to Mother led to arguments, head shaking, and diligent efforts to find a more suitable church for me.

 I picked up teachings that rubbed somebody the wrong way and made me feel as if I'd done something horrible by repeating what I thought Divine Truth. Dancing turned out to be a cataclysmic confrontation because Ida loved music and attended dances at the American Legion hall in Arbordale. I was shocked the first time they took me, and sat in silence with children at wood tables along the wall as grown ups danced across the hard plank floor while the band, consisting of a piano, banjo, trumpet, tuba, and a trombone played by a man who also beat a drum with a foot pedal, thumped tunes. Men sipped vile whiskey from bottles in paper bags, and sneaked to the porch to smoke. I was bearing witness to sinning through intoxication and maybe even fornication.

 I became sullen and disturbed during the ride back to the farm in Grandpa's Lincoln, a remnant of better days before the Great Depression when he was a farm equipment salesman. It was when Grandma was tucking me into bed that I began to cry. She asked what was wrong. It took considerable coaxing before I said they were going to Hell and it made me sad. For a time they didn't send me to Sunday school; it made no practical difference in my life. I rejoined my mother in Jamestown, North Dakota. When I asked about church, she said it wasn't important. Through some boys in third grade I learned about a church I hadn't attended--Catholic. According to them, it was the one true church, and everybody else was going straight to Hell. That didn't seem right, and I resisted what they asserted as best I could. Turned out I was what they called an unredeemed Protestant, one of the worst and most-to-be-pitied sinners on earth, and was doomed to spend time in some underground place called Purgatory. It sounded like one of the filthy bus stations or train terminals I'd been through, not very comfortable, and I'd have to pray for a better place after my sins were washed away. I complained to my mother about sending me to false churches.

She wanted to know what I was talking about. I told about the Catholic Church, that it was the only way to get to Heaven and, furthermore, if I happened to sin and put my soul in danger, I could explain it all to a priest and get cleansed. That set her off, and she bawled me out. I was overwhelmed as she railed about Catholics and the Pope, who persecuted good Christians while the monks and nuns carried on and threw babies down wells. I had no idea what she was talking about, but it came to me that my church years were a waste since I couldn't figure things out if grownups, who must know the truth of things, thrashed me every which way.

Mother settled on sending me to Methodist or Lutheran Sunday school, but one day when I was nine and flush with power, I picked a fight and told her I wanted to be a Catholic. I didn't, but it was my way of putting the weird business aside and getting on with my life. That's the first time I recall consciously manipulating her for my own good, but not the last. As I sat in Sunday school listening to blather about living a good life, I counter-argued in my mind. If I raised tough questions or sought reasonable answers, it led to a note home.

After a time, Sunday school class was dropped; Mom found them more trouble than my religious education was worth.

I don't know why it is after so many decades, but I still find myself curious about faiths and beliefs. I sought answers majoring in Philosophy and Comparative Religion during college, but found both fields unsatisfying. I've attended many churches just to be in the presence of dedicated practitioners, and I sometimes feel that I am monitoring their progress. When moved, I can proclaim 'Glory be' and 'Hallelujah' with fervent Pentecostals or Evangelicals, but remain aloof from heartfelt conviction. It was fate to be nurtured in a spiritual cafeteria offering excess choice and universal mystery. I married a sweet Presbyterian, who told me when the time comes to go the Heaven I should simply hang on tight to the hem of her robe. Shortest and best sermon I ever heard, and therefore the most satisfying, by God.

CATACOMBING

I t was like a coal mine without coal, that sub-basement of the seventy-year-old brick building, dark and dank, mildew dust with a crusted stench of flaking mortar, and lined with warped plank file shelves. After my first week on the third floor where clerks shuffled locomotive service files, the chief clerk, Mr. Morse, assigned me to destroy ancient files. Although he didn't wear a green eyeshade or cuff guards, he still looked quite fusty.

We got to an oak door on the first floor, which he unlocked with a skeleton key. Then we descended into a crypt. I thought we had reached the place, but he paced to a rusted iron door. It opened like a vault, down more stairs into file storage hell. He snapped on a light switch. Amber bulbs blazed on an electrical cord strung along the ceiling.

"Just what am I'm supposed to do?" I asked.

"Here's a list. Keep most files only ten years.."

He handed me the sheet listing over a hundred subjects from Accidents, General through Locomotive Repair, General to Waybills. My job was to examine each file and trash the old. Mr. Morse indicated two empty oil drums by the door for the discards.

"How far back do these files go?"

"Let's see." He pulled one from a shelf, blowing dust and shaking cobwebs off. "Mid-1923 through 1938. Yup-- this one can be pitched."

"You said the longest time to keep them was ten years."

"It's been quite a while since these were culled out."

"My God, sir. This will take months."

"Not so bad. The thing is...." He looked for a file. "See how this starts in 1930 and ends 1953--last year. You save only since 1943."

He put the file back and left. It was eight thirty, three hours to lunch; my brown bag sat by the file clerk's desk on the third floor. A light spilled into my prison from a grated window. I took a three-leg stool to the end of the room, stood on it, and stared. Through the ground-level window I saw an olive tree, a chain link fence by the tracks, and Los Angeles sky. It was a nice, more natural view than the sooty repair shops viewed from the third floor.

During my first hour there was little to engage my spirit and I felt the despair that isolated prisoners must suffer. I began with Accidents, General, foul packets dating back half a century. It took hours to discard everything but the last ten years. Feeling as musty as my prison, I traipsed upstairs for lunch. Seated at a railroad salvage oak desk in the file room, there was no one to talk to. Everyone retreated into their cocoon with magazines and books. The rest of the day I numbly checked dates, chucked files, and scratched off completed categories on the list. By mid-week I was stupefied and considered quitting.

Then I got to Accidents, Reports covering every crossing collision from San Francisco to New Orleans. Printed in blue ink, it was a history of mishap and calamity. In 1913, my attention was caught by the initial report. *Hay wagon in Texas. Hit by a freight train. Deceased: Arvidal Fraits, 59. Hay wagon destroyed. Steam engine undamaged but crossing sign demolished by debris. Engineer sounded warning but wagon didn't move despite repeated whistle blasts. Driver didn't whip the horses to remove wagon from tracks. Both horses survived in a field nibbling alfalfa.*

An old man, dead. Why didn't he urge the horses to pull the wagon across? Was he deaf? Asleep? Did he have a stroke? Why weren't the horses scared enough by the whistle to bolt out of danger? My thoughts were suffused with mystery. The next day, I took my lunch to the crypt so I could read while eating.

The variety of death and destruction at railroad crossings began to intoxicate me. Maybe I was desperate given the tedious work. Soon it was clear that I was visiting a tragic cavalcade--ordinary people having mortal encounters. Each day I reported in to Mr. Morse before going to my deep cloister. I hid my enthusiasm as he apologized for the drudgery and encouraged me. Because I wanted to read more and work less, I ravaged other files quick to pitch or save so I could peruse accident reports. I was able to pace myself, show Mr. Morse progress, but spend much of the day reading.

The reports for 1917-18 reflected a change. There were frequent accidents that involved motor vehicles--both trucks and cars, a few small busses. And more men in uniform. Typical: *Private Joel Rutcher, Model T Ford, totally demolished. He and a female passenger killed; ages nineteen and sixteen. Car raced train along gravel road to the crossing. Collision occurred at approximately twenty-five miles per hour.* A young soldier in the full rush of manhood, showing off for his girl? Drinking maybe? Jousting against the smoke and steam monster?

I never knew when Mr. Morse would check on me, so I placed one barrel in the doorway. When he moved it to get in I was alerted. That gave me a few seconds to hide the file I read and grab one to either toss or keep. In an eight-hour shift I read for six and worked for two. I became so engrossed that it was a month before it occurred to me that I was addicted. Reports during the 1920s reflected a fatalism that I associated with the times: a 'Roaring' decade of fast cars and booze with increased casualties.

Miss Evangeline Langer, twenty three, driving a large Hudson touring sedan loaded with sorority sisters near San Diego. None of that insane male racing to beat the train, but equally disturbing. Parked on the tracks waiting for a train to speed toward them. Testimony from the survivor, a collegian like myself, thrown clear as five others were crushed to death in the car. They'd been drinking and smoking, parked on the crossing after midnight. They took turns behind the wheel; when a train came, the driver had to start the car and wait till just before the train was upon them before driving off. One of them, deceased, jammed the gearbox.

The more I read and slaved in that subterranean chamber, the more it came to me how little I knew about life and death. My college major was undecided, but my interest was history. Whatever human life was supposed to be about from the few classics I had read, it was clear that all a person had was each instant and what had passed before as a memory. I felt like a secluded monk paging archives. Time faded into a mist as I visited tragic, empty lives. How precious life was--to breathe, eat, sleep, work, think, and feel. *Essence.*

As I threw myself into purging expendable files, it was a joyous physical release. Sweat soaked my T-shirt and bathed me in a delicious weariness. Mr. Morse thanked me for my hard work; often he sent a clerk down with cola or root beer; said I was the hardest student they had ever had. I felt guilty, two hours work in eight. The 1930s reports were a revelation. It was clear to me, a crossing accident expert, that there was a change in victim motivation.

Forty-five-year-old Davis Murchison, father of three, unemployed more than five years when he encountered a fifty-mile-an-hour passenger locomotive in his Chevrolet. He was alone, as were most fellow decedents during that decade. He approached the crossing deliberately, it appeared to the engineer, either increasing speed or slowing as distance narrowed, until the auto and locomotive met in fiery finality. Despite the terse administrative jargon, it was clear that Mr. Murchison meant to kill himself. Was it for insurance? To be less of a burden to his family? An act of despair with no way out?

Through August into the first week of September I read like a fiend, unable to get my fill of the various calamities that had afflicted so many fellow human beings. Nothing before or since has had the same effect. I devoured deathly tales past the 1943 pitch date, having absorbed the tone and style so well that I could conclude the post mortem before the end: *A school bus with fifteen lives exploded into catastrophe for themselves and their parents; three boys racing an engine along the tracks on their bicycles before vibration from the railroad ties disoriented them and they were run down like animals; a motorcycle with sidecar, sergeant driver and major riding, the major killed instantly, the sergeant dragged under the engine a mile until unrecognizable as a human being.*

I worked the four extra days after Labor Day. Mr. Morse, after inspecting the lean shelves of my solitary labyrinth, declared that nobody had ever worked so hard at such a dreary job and done it so well. He didn't know that culling the death files had brought me to life. We had cake and punch my last day. I chatted amiably with the alien clerks as fellow travelers whose lives and concerns would pass. We lived in triviality, dealt with it, and treasured mere few moments. What began as a drudge duty was a blessed salvation. Years later I came upon some musty reports that I had salvaged from their oblivion and was tempted to reread them. Instead, chastened by time, I sanctified my long-ago innocent task by pitching them into eternity.

THE MOUNTAIN TRAIL

You read about the death of movie star kids often enough that it is routine tabloid news. Cory Rogers death from cocaine overdose set off emotions with images of pristine sky, crisp air and an aura of pines with the creak of saddle leather and smell of sweaty horses. *Only son of starlet Lilianne Cory and actor Greg Rogers' first of three marriages. Cory Rogers, forty-two, ex-wife and teen daughter. He was in movies in the 1960s, TV in the 1970s, and directed in the 1980s.* Cory had finally ridden over the precipice.

Thirty-two years back, summer '53, I traveled by train from Los Angeles to Flagstaff, a twenty-year-old camp counselor with my first job out of the army. I was a high school dropout with two years in Japan and Korea, too old to be a kid but too young to be an adult. I tried for the summer job in a posh boys camp at fifty dollars a week plus room and board. Fred Riddle, owner and manager of Indian Camps, hired eight college-age guys to oversee eighty sons of show biz celebrities. I'd lied, claiming I could ride horses. Fred sensed it, but liked my army service rise from private to sergeant and campaign medals, or maybe he was just sorry for an errant soul.

At Union Station before departure, I met my tribe of ten boys, checked off names as they jostled, goosed, and punched each other in their Levis and Indian Camps T-shirts. Cory's mother looked familiar but I didn't make the connection to his dad, Gregory, who I'd seen in westerns and war movies. Lilianne Cory Rogers was a freckled, perky blonde, and held her cigarette aside when she hugged her son. She shook my hand as I promised her I'd look after Cory. On the train ride, I strained to handle boys half my age, trying to be both leader and friend. They pestered me about my army life as we arm wrestled and caroused. Cory was strong, petulant, cynical and, he looked like his dad--severe.

Two weeks after arriving at camp on a mountain plateau in the heart of Coconino County, Cory and I were confined to the dispensary with chicken pox. When Cory came down with it, Fred Riddle asked the counselors if we'd had it and I said I had--but that wasn't true either. As we lay daubed with calamine lotion, I wanted to understand him better since he'd been trouble, picking fights with my Choctaw tribe kids.

He was also reckless, particularly during canoeing on the lake below the meadow where the plank cabins of the camp were situated like a frontier fort. He paddled toward the log dam over which water surged down into to Oak Creek Canyon. I kept him with me so he wouldn't endanger others. Much as I hated chicken pox, lazing about was great, even if it meant sharing the room with Cory. He was sullen and sassed the nurse, Imogene, a stolid Navaho from the University in Flagstaff who tried to baby him. At night, Cory's pathological demons emerged.

He had nightmares. Not the normal, fretful dreams of ten-year-olds, but convulsions with groaning and whimpering. One night he half-turned in the bed so that his muscular frame draped precariously. I got up to help so he wouldn't fall. He threw both arms around me and held on with such tenacity that I couldn't break free. I sat on his bed and eased him down till we were side by side, his soft brown hair against my face. I'm not sure how long we stayed like that, but I kept waking as he groaned for somebody to stop whatever was being done to him.

When healthy again, we weren't exactly friends, but had a tacit understanding of some kind. Cory never accepted my casual consoling, but he stopped provoking other boys and obeyed the rules of the tribe. This change came at the price of silence. He only spoke when asked to and became the somber warrior of the Choctaws. Neither taunted nor teased, he was a stolid brave in the camp's youthful tribalism.

Cory was good at everything: archery, baseball, hiking, canoeing, wrestling, boxing and crafts--braiding, beading, leather working. But what he was best at was riding. The first day back on duty was my tribe's turn with horses. After breakfast we went to the stables. I had met 'Raz' Rasmussen, the wrangler. The other counselors were saddle hands, and when Raz asked, I said I'd done some riding at stables near Griffith Park. Actually, I'd had one ride into the park and never made my stable-plug nag obey.

In the corral there were a dozen horses waiting to be saddled. Two of my boys and Cory grabbed saddles, pads, and bridles, and started to work. I watched them and Raz, who helped the smaller boys. He gazed my way as I tossed a pad on what looked to be the gentlest horse. Before I could lift the saddle onto its back, Raz rambled over shaking his head, his bowlegged gait as measured as a crusty old cowhand could be, and spat into the dust. Grit-gray hair dangled below the grimed straw hat. He grouched 'Damn' and 'Collige bastids' plaguing his old age. Lugging the pad to another horse, he grabbed the saddle with one hand and hoisted it up and taught me to cinch it. Then he had me bridle the horse, guffawing when yellow teeth nipped at my fingers.

The two-hour ride angled into the meadow along the lake before trailing onto pine and cedar slopes till we left the camp behind and were swallowed by wilderness. Raz had the lead, followed single file by Choctaws while I stayed back to prod laggards. Keeping the small boys moving didn't let me enjoy the grandeur as the trail emerged from a thick stand of pines into Oak Creek Canyon. Sandstone bluffs, molded by wind and water, glowed orange in the sun.

The trail snaked along a ridge but soon became dips and rises like a roller coaster till, from behind, we looked like an awkward beast with T-shirted creatures mounted on a primordial beast with forty-eight legs. We left patches of warm sunshine as shadow and chill engulfed us. After dropping a few hundred feet, the trail went up into hairpin turns as the front of our group came to a steep rise with a blind corner. The trail was six feet wide, with a drop on the right.

Raz told the boys in his gruff voice as he spat tobacco juice into the dust, to move fast and jerk the reins left across the horse's neck right before the turn. Not too quick or the horse might spook, slam into the rock wall and lose its footing. He spurred his horse up through the corner. Cory did too, but I sensed he wanted to show off and rode fast, twisting the reins at the last instant to avoid plunging off the trail.

Two boys managed the maneuver with minor awkwardness, and as the rest of us neared I began to have trouble breathing, just like the first few high altitude days, trying to catch a life-sustaining breath. Besides my duty to keep the smaller boys moving, I was worried about my ability to manage the turn. I tried to appear confidant with my Choctaws as they babbled and squealed, and finally trotted over the rise and out of sight.

HUNCHING HOMEWARD

I stalled, hoping my horse would do what he'd done with other riders. But he became sluggish. I gazed at the bend of the trail and heard a voice urging me ahead--Raz, echoed by Cory and the Choctaws. In desperation I dug my boot heels into the horse's flanks. He lurched, almost tossing me off as I clutched the horn, sensing in panic that I wouldn't be able to veer left by dragging the reins across his neck. With breathtaking speed, we whipped around the turn and pulled up at the waiting tribe. Raz smiled, spat, and said that it was a good thing he'd put me on a quarter horse smarter than any human that ever lived.

After that, with me still struggling to breathe steadily, we drifted through the high ridges till popping out of the pines a mile below the camp. It was midday and the horses, sensing we were heading home where water and rest waited, picked up speed. Raz made the boys rein back, but they wanted to gallop. He resisted, spat a tobacco gob, and gazed back at the column, his eyes pinched in weathered, crinkled folds of skin. Cory spurred his horse into a trot, canter, and gallop. The eager, yelling Choctaws thundered after him.

My horse strained to join the cavalry charge. I reined back as he leapt to follow the boys. Terrified, I hung on as his hoofs beat the ground in a brain-numbing cadence. Wheezing gasps brushed my face as I leaned while holding the reins so tight both hands ached. Surprise! At a gallop the ride was smooth and thrilling. I passed the slowest, then another and Raz till I was ahead of Cory. The horse leaped a stream and slowed to a trot near the stable. The Choctaws reined up, shouting about my ride. It was hosted at lunch with Kool Aid and banging spoons.

During an Indian war game where my Choctaws had to pursue another tribe into the forest, I walked behind the boys, watching for roots and other hazards. Agile Cory ran ahead, whooping like a true savage, and then stopped. When we caught up, he stood three feet from a coiled rattlesnake. We stared in morbid paralysis. Cory, holding a spear with a plastic point, poked the snake and lifted it up despite my warning. The snake, two feet of writhing anger, kept slithering off the spear. Cory got a baseball-sized rock and hurled it at the snake with such fury it was soon dead, its rattle silent. We hurried on with the war game, awestruck by Cory.

Two weeks before camp ended, on another ride into Oak Creek Canyon, we came to a new trail, rougher than any we had ridden before. By then the boys were good riders. I was also more confident, and Raz, who carried a flask of rye, sometimes rode off trail for a snort. But I wasn't complacent about Cory. As we reached a tricky turn in the trail, he insisted on galloping. He spurred the horse toward the cutback in the trail. My horse shot after. Cory was only one length ahead when time to rein over. His horse flatfooted and lurched, its back legs off the trail. It reared. Cory leaned forward. For an instant horse and boy hung in space, the animal straining wildly to gain a footing. I sped ahead, fearing the collision that would hurl us over the edge. My horse slammed Cory's. Both animals neighed, snorted, and scrambled through the turn.

As we reined up behind the waiting Choctaws and Raz, I was trembling and knew I must look bloodless. Cory turned about, flushed and angry that I had followed too close. He raged at me, spurred his horse about savagely, and galloped back down the trail. I was so stunned it took a moment before I realized Cory's shout meant that he was making another run at the turn in the trail. He came on so fast that his horse's hoofs crumbled the edge of the trail, kicking rocks into the canyon. He rode through, pulled up, wiped his sweaty face, eased past at a walk, and then cantered to the top of the ridge.

Raz and I brought up the rear without a word, he taking occasional swigs from his bottle. Cory led the column back to camp. Raz uttered 'Damned foolishness' and 'Dumb stunt.' It was the last time my Choctaws rode through Oak Creek Canyon, the final time Cory courted danger. The return trip to Los Angeles was wistful because I felt a kinship with the boys who had spent their precious ten-year-old selves with me. It reminded me how quickly my own childhood had passed without much to remember.

I expected Cory's mother, Lilianne, at the station. Instead I met a middle-aged man with shaggy hair, mottled facial skin, and a lax way of standing. He wore sunglasses; it was Gregory Rogers, movie star, but not very heroic in stature. I said it was a thrill to meet him and Cory had been a swell camper. He shook my hand, gripped Cory's arm and led him off. Cory gazed back, again a stranger with deep-set eyes. Over the years I noted stories about his life during my own mundane existence. His death became a memory of almost falling over the edge of oblivion. I haven't ridden a horse since that summer.

WHEN GODS WALK THE EARTH

After Miles Barton Kuperman was arrested on Santa Monica Beach for accosting three underage girls in string bikinis, it brought back bittersweet memories of babysitting him when he was a twenty-four-year-old account executive. It was my second advertising job after getting an MBA, and it took eighteen weeks to learn that it wasn't a fast track to the big time. I joined an agency with closet skeletons and a succession issue disguised as a handsome heir-apparent.

Frisch Kuperman & Caffey was an old-line agency with a half dozen flagship accounts anchored by a prominent mortgage bank and bolstered by a medium-sized oil company, upscale department store, modest cruise line sailing the Mexican Riviera, and a cloth napkin restaurant whose best copy point said that it served your dinner salad with a chilled fork. The remaining clients were minor retail and service accounts attached to the agency teams for cash flow.

HUNCHING HOMEWARD

The stealth client was a Las Vegas resort-casino known as the Palmetto before renamed the Socorro, a holdover from the early days when the agency also performed mystery projects for Howard Hughes. The Creative Director, Gary Caffey, regaled us boozing acolytes with tales of waiting in the agency's Cadillac at various rendezvous spots on Mulholland Drive with copy and layout for the great man's approval. At the appointed hour, a limo would arrive and, after a once-over by bodyguards, Gary would be escorted into the back seat, remain silent in the presence of majesty, and return later with scrawled initials of approval.

Known as Fresh Kuppa Coffee in the business, F K & C was envied for its fifteen percent commissions and considered antiquated when more progressive clients negotiated discounts and assigned freelancers for media and market research. The agency remained as genteel and formal as the storied relationships between founding heads of advertising agencies and client CEOs in the Good-Old-Boy days.

An inept account exec like Miles survived in F K & C's relaxed deadwood clan under the most idyllic arrangement. Irene Kuperman, Mile's mother, widow of Maddox Kuperman, made it possible. She held fifty-five percent of the stock, making nepotism official policy. Sol Frisch, Maddox's partner, went along to protect his twenty five percent, Gary Caffey had fifteen; the last five percent was doled out to senior executives for servile behavior. I received the promise of a bonus as a junior account exec. Had I been more alert during the job interview I'd have noted the icy-blonde woman chain-smoking in back as Sol Frisch schmoozed and might've surmised that Irene was more than an aging model.

The snide judgment about Miles among the staff, especially the Creatives, said that he was so dumb all the other account guys knew it. When I first heard that, it struck me as cruel since he looked like a near-perfect ad exec--tall, lithe, blonde, blue-eyed, with a sensual mouth you knew would photograph with that I-don't-give-a-damn-about-you pout of models in men's fashion mags. Also, he walked with a graceful gait as if a runner had slowed to admire the world. Poised in the hallway, he seemed like a statue, perhaps a youth from ancient days. The problem: there was nothing there, the epitome of the 'empty suit' epithet from colleagues.

I was efficient enough at my initial assignments involving tersely-written contact reports and budgets that I garnered Sol Frisch's notice. He brought me aside one Friday afternoon, tan in his golf shirt with sun lines splayed about his blue eyes and tufts of white hair coiffed over each ear. He praised me for my first four months and assigned me to the bank client with Miles--not consumer advertising but rather the business-to-business campaign in the trade magazines. I caught on that it was a task where Miles couldn't create difficulties since Sol socialized the bank's president and Irene Kuperman had fifty thousand shares of bank stock. Sol thought my laid-back style would wear well with Irene Kuperman's golden son. He made no bones about what my job was; keep the guy from screwing up.

After the meeting I confronted Miles in his corner office, a plush perk reserved for senior execs, and told him I had been assigned to that group. He was buddy-buddy and said we should celebrate by going out for drinks. It was early afternoon and his desk was clear because he didn't have a lot to do. We went to the South Seas bar off the lobby of our West L. A. office building with its sober overview of the VA Cemetery. Gazing upon a park of headstones didn't fill me with somber thoughts of mortality so much as the more benign notion that it wasn't a bad place to spend eternity. Miles lounged in the booth and gulped two Mai Tais brought by the hula-skirt barmaid without being asked. The drinks didn't alter his baritone delivery, which was like a child reciting, hollow.

What made it so strange was that he looked terrific, not movie star handsome, but well turned. As he gazed about the cocktail lounge, nodding when someone passed by, I felt as if in the presence of a celebrity. Girls taking a smoke and drink break at another table stared at us. Miles radiated a natural glow as he mumbled inanities about the bank's print campaign, which I ignored till the conversation shifted to complaints. He bemoaned not getting meaningful work, bitching to Sol about it, being put off, and vowing to tell his mother. When he did, Irene told him it took time to learn the business and he must be patient. The more I listened, the first time I'd been with him in private, the more it was hard to believe that Irene Kuperman, even with Sol's help, thought the future of F K & C could ever rest in Miles' hands.

Drinking with him became a once-or-twice weekly ritual, following the same path of Mai Tais and bitching. If it was Friday and other agency folks swung by to juice before going home, Miles picked up drink tabs. They were happy to drink his money and escape to more rewarding repartee. It seemed to be my task to remain with him, as Sol explained when I told him I was having a hard time keeping Miles steady. Sol said it was part of my job, and gave me a raise.

At the first half-year progress dinner reporting on financial status, I was not only invited, the sole junior account exec present, but seated across from Miles at the banquet table beside the dowager herself, Irene. She wore a beige tailored suit, diamond-studded necklace and Mandarin-red silk blouse, with an armory of bracelets, rings and brooches. Miles perched on Sol's right, who occupied the table head, Irene at Sol's left, and myself. During dinner, after glowing profit reports and mid-year bonuses, I received an envelope with a twenty percent bonus on my first six months salary.

I gasped. Irene gazed at me with feral green eyes. I shivered thinking I had done something terrible. 'Problem?' she said through lips open just enough to let the word out. I shook my head and tried to grasp what made me so much more valuable to F K & C than other junior account execs. As if reading my mind, Irene said, 'Keep up the good work with Miles.'

What, I wondered during the meal, was I doing for, and with, Miles that was deemed so valuable? Over the next few weeks it occurred to me that I had become something of a playmate. In addition to drinking with him and holding down the passenger seat in his silver Corvette, I was required to spend night and weekend time as a sort of sidekick-cum-buddy. This involved driving around and drinking in restaurants and clubs as he complained about his miserable life. What I recall between bouts of boozing, moderate on my part, was whining and moaning about his father, Maddox, one son-of-a-bitch, and his mother, a devil who could rip the heart out of a great white shark. Being raised by predator parents was the primal theme.

The oddest part of this relationship was Miles' complete disregard for women. To say that he was an object of intense curiosity from a bevy of females understates the case. Wherever we pub-crawled he was the center of attention while women eyed him with sly smiles, winks, pursed lips, giggles, and jealous glances from their male dates. Just who the hell was he, guys' sardonic looks seemed to convey, to be so damned gifted with godlike features? Who indeed? Miles Barton Kuperman, prince regent to a business that wouldn't survive his tenure a year. It was a reminder that hereditary kingship had been done in, not by revolution, but by the genetic vagaries of sons and grandsons.

Ah, the women, bitches in his estimation; voracious creatures whose sole mission in life appeared to be domination. At first it bothered me that he was content with male friendship and that perhaps I was to be his paramour. Thinking back, that notion was moronic. He was neither hetero-nor-homo, but asexual. There was no lust in him. Had he been a statue, he wouldn't have been marble or granite but a plaster shell like a fashion manikin. When drink made him morose and misogynistic, he was most angry about a life that seemed senseless.

His cynicism played itself out during the agency's summer beach party hosted at the posh Pacifican Club, an opulent white wood remnant of a 1920s Hollywood beach house. The chance to party in members-only affluence was heady for the secretaries and media gals who noshed and played bikini volleyball with inebriated abandon. I didn't grasp the extent of Miles' disgust with females till several tried to coax him onto the dance floor amid cavorting and bouncing couples who exhibited a frenzy of gyrating flesh.

Miles jerked away from two laughing girls who were trying to drag him out there. One fell backwards into a food table with a squeal as the other hung onto his shirt until it ripped. He shoved her and she reeled through dancing couples, her squeal lost in the DJ's raucous records till she was caught before falling by two account execs clutching cans of beer. I couldn't hear what she yelled, but her lips formed words reasonably rendered as 'fag,' 'queer,' and the more prosaic, 'shit.'

He left the club to lurch away down the beach toward the public area, his tan legs below tennis shorts straining muscularly through the sand as his body flexed like a dissolute athlete trying to outrun pursuing hounds. I hesitated going after him the instant I recalled my official status as a nanny was an embarrassment and making me self-conscious about not being a full-fledged junior exec. Peers at F K & C were moving ahead with true ad projects while I'd been shunted into an inane responsibility. Sol Frisch and Irene were at a table in the far corner of the verandah, looking like either conspirators or aging lovers sharing a stolen moment. They were grim-faced as Miles departed. I imagined it might be a reaction to my having not prevented his outrageous behavior. I slunk to the bar for a vodka-rocks and tried to be invisible while mulling my very thin resume.

That lasted perhaps a half hour until I found myself being escorted upstairs to the game room with billiard tables, leather chairs, and a picture window the entire length of the second floor that revealed the sun-drenched amber ocean rippling toward the Orient. Sol sat me down, mumbled a few pleasantries about how things were going, and got to the matter at hand--Miles. Could I stick, keep an eye on him? I wanted to protect a pay package beyond my wildest hopes but lamented that I'd fallen off the career track. In a manner I'd often seen him use to mollify a client when F K & C botched a project, he gave me a brief history of Miles Barton Kuperman.

The boy had often been pummeled in a rage by Maddox, and Irene doted on him. There must be brain damage, because the kid had never performed well in school despite tutoring, prep school, and an arranged diploma from Stanford. It was a hell of a problem, and Sol and Irene were trying to build a team around Miles that would sustain F K & C's competitive stature. They had hoped that I might be one of those key executives. It was quite an admission, and I thanked him for leveling with me, but said I wasn't sure it was a task I could do. What I didn't tell him was that Miles scared me with his outbursts. Sol appeared to understand, with a sadness that made his persuasive features go slack, but asked me to think about it. I did, but decided that I wasn't suited to serve a boy-god, attractive as the financial riches appeared. I resigned to go to the branch office of a national agency, but kept an eye on F K & C through contacts.

The story that played out was Miles on one of his jaunts on Santa Monica beach coming upon three drugged-out girls looking for a good-time stud. They made the mistake trying to feel him up. Miles punched one of them in the face. Screams and shouts brought a cop who, trying to untangle Miles from the girls, got mauled by an out-of-control Miles. It needed three officers to subdue him with clubs to the head. Those blows devastated his face and knocked circuits loose in the brain. I lost track of the legal aspects of the case and assumed that it was settled off-stage as are most such issues that involve moneyed people.

F K & C was acquired a few years later by a major agency. Sol retired. Irene stayed a patron of the arts and served on corporate and charitable boards. I never heard anything more about Miles Barton Kuperman except rumors that he was actually the son of Sol and Irene. I suppose that's possible, but it made no difference to me. Miles ended up in a plush sanitarium near Palm Springs, a place where money takes good care of people with personal problems. My life and career, mundane as they were, ambled modestly beyond mortal deities.

STORIES TOLD, LIES DENIED

When Tod Rankin first met Risa Blaine in a St. Louis singles bar during the 1973 Fourth of July bash, he sold himself as the Senior Marketing Manager for Mid-Western Foods, Incorporated's grocery brands that included ready-to-eat cereals, pet foods, frozen entrees, sea foods such as tuna, crab, salmon and shrimp, and various institutional items for bulk feeding. She explained that she was Group Account Executive at Rutters & Beckelmann Advertising Agency handling Trans-West Airlines, Missouri Underwriters Insurance, and other important clients not worth mentioning in the meat-market socializing frenzy of the River Barge Saloon.

They were both lying to impress each other, which was expected within the overheated and lusting milieu, but managed in the course of a half dozen vodka-tonics to convey at least one truth to each other, trivial though it seemed--that his full name was Todley Wilmette Rankin III, which Risa at once characterized as Todley Winks, and that her *euphonious appellation* (screen credit due W. C. Field's reply to Mae West in *My Little Chickadee*) was Marisa Hazelton Blaine. It was immediately apparent that they hailed from ultra-societal parentage, certainly didn't have to work at anything if they chose not to, and may have fortuitously caromed into their one-and-only soul-mate. They went to a posh hotel suite and screwed each other's brains out.

It was over the course of the next few weeks and months that they learned the full extent of their systematic deception. Tod was actually only the product manager for dog foods, and Risa was an account executive on Missouri Valley Hardware. The truth did not dismay either of them since they thrived on personal and social lies as a compulsive pastime. Furthermore, they could, without the unseemliest sign of remorse, even extend their various deceits beyond each other at parties where they indulged their peculiar habit without fear of disclosure.

It helped enormously that they looked the part of most outrageous tales they selected to tell. Tod was athletically tall and blonde, with a men's catalog demeanor and fulsome baritone that permitted him to pass as a film or television actor even if an audience had reason to suspect his grotesque exaggerations and name-droppings. Risa wasn't beautiful in the same flashy way that Tod was handsome, but she had a vivacity and insouciance that made her charming to such an extent that when she related having given up a modeling career in Chicago (where she had done a few photo-sessions as a teen while at Archer Academy For Girls), it was credible. Tod and Risa were, in essence, perfectly type cast to journey through life in any improvisational guise they chose to perform.

Their colleagues at work were on to them, of course, and kidded both with a ruthless savagery mitigated only by Tod and Risa's opulent trust funds which gave them the resources to host drinking bouts and dinner parties at lavish expense and hold a coterie of passionate hangers-on at a moment's notice. There is nothing quite so luxurious and intoxicating as a guaranteed audience for one's fantasies. In time, it was assumed, that they would marry and settle down-- which they did, buying one of the most prestigious penthouse condominiums in Chateau Beau Monde overlooking the Mississippi River. They also achieved higher status in their respective companies, not due to any innate marketing or advertising abilities, but because they had an old-money style that served them well in the *nouveau panache* that clung to the business community. There is, in almost every human commercial enterprise, an opportunity for role-playing and set decoration, and both Tod and Risa played their professional parts with dramaturgical flair.

By the time they were in their forties, however, and had acquired the wearying effects of early middle age--wrinkles from extravagant tropical vacations that no cosmetic tightening could permanently alleviate, a vacuous stare from matching blue-gray eyes that increasingly seemed so lifeless, and a slackness of flesh that no amount of exercise and frantic, huffing games of tennis could offset, combined with gallons of liquor consumed over decades—an abyss opened before them: they were becoming garishly ridiculous. Their circle of acquaintances they'd drawn-upon over many years began to dwindle, the parties waned in satisfaction, and the love affairs (real or unreal) no longer carried the same excitement. In brief, the mid-life crisis Tod and Risa Rankin arrived at simultaneously devastated their enfeebled spirits.

Thus it became necessary to enhance the one character trait that had taken them so far in their personal and business careers--they began to systematically, rather than spontaneously, tell stories about themselves that went far beyond the socially permissible little exaggerations they had so mischievously indulged in for years. Where once Tod had jokingly claimed to have been trained as an amateur bullfighter during a summer-long visit to Mexico as a teenager, he began, when given a chance during a cocktail party, extolling his exploits for more than half an hour to enthralled guests who had never before heard his wild tales. Often he added fillips of the exotic, such as falling in love with the ravishing daughter of Don Luis Somebody-or-other at whose lush *hacienda* he had stayed. He was careful enough to have read Hemingway in order to speak with superficial authority about the intricacies of the sport, and could convincingly express details of *corrida, banderillas,* and *paseos* with aplomb.

For her part, Risa's adventures, were equally engaging, the most risque being a rafting trip on the Orinoco that involved encounters, both funny and scary, with headhunters, pythons, and feminine rituals where she was required to paint her naked body with gross pigments and perform a sexual initiation dance before a horde of chanting warriors. Neither Tod nor Risa became cavalier about what was expected of them; they studied and discussed their respective fabulosities until assured that they could carry them off with total conviction, often rehearsing lines upon one another and critiquing phrases and effects. While it was essential to their self-image that they be acceptably credible, they didn't believe their own lies beyond mustering emotional energy to perform; they were actors, and sought only suspension of disbelief.

They were invited to parties solely because hosts expected them to be vastly amusing in their peculiar style. It was, however, inevitable that they might on some occasion encounter if not a hostile or cynical audience, at least an indifferent one. At a party in the mid-1990's, Tod was artfully-launched on one of his more flamboyant follies, the occasion when, as a teenager, he had climbed the Matterhorn and nearly fallen to his death in his zeal to photograph every thrilling moment of the ascent. He had been cautioned by the guide, but in his youthful exuberance he'd grown careless (it always lent special credibility to their sagas if Tod and Risa might somehow claim a personal culpability for whatever calamity they experienced) and placed his foot on a ledge of rock which gave way. He dangled over the edge of a thousand foot Alpine chasm.

As Tod related his rescue by the guide and other climbers, he was aware of the cryptic stare of one of the guests, a leather-faced man with a shag of gray hair and appearance of an outdoorsman. Suddenly sensing he might be endangered, he muted the closure and gulped his drink as if in relief at having cheated death so many years before. Other guests smiled at the novelty of the adventure, but the stalwart man merely asked a technical question having to do with climbing cleats and the tethering rope. Tod fumbled an answer, took a deep draught, and felt the vodka sear his throat as he tried to smile and laugh off the near-disaster implicit in his story. The man persisted with further questions: what time of year had the incident taken place? How many in the climbing party? Did Tod continue the climb to the summit?

The more Tod equivocated and shimmied around the answers, the more he realized some of the dozen or so guests who had attentively listened were drifting away to other groups. When there were only two couples left besides the craggy inquisitor, Tod shrugged as if to say that he was just glad it had all been a long time ago and he was no longer so young and foolish and had, in fact, not climbed any peaks since. It was a deferential maneuver designed to deflect any more probing. The man who had unaccountably pinioned him, snorted, and said that he didn't believe a word of what Tod had related. He was a climber and went so far as to proclaim that Tod may never have even seen the Matterhorn, let alone climbed it. Tod was not drunk, but he flushed, and in a surge of bilish rage, called the heckler a son of a bitch, and goddamned liar.

The man smiled with massively white teeth and crinkly eyes, conveying such a facade of unruffled confidence, that Tod flushed even more, his hands shaking as sweat poured from both armpits. He gestured with his half-filled glass, thinking in a mad moment to hurl it into the man's face, but was restrained when Risa arrived to ask how everyone was doing. Tod barely managed a welcoming smile for her as she immediately grasped that his performance was not going well. Before Tod could engage the man further, he was assailed with an accusation of his falsehood that made him grip the glass so tight he hoped it would shatter, sever a vein, and spew blood to distract from his shame and validate, in a histrionic way, his manhood. Risa weaved her hand through his arm, smiled at the attacker, and steered Tod away.

They left when convenient to do so without provoking special notice. In their Cadillac, Risa attempted to placate Tod, telling him that some people were simply too discourteous and uncivilized to accept the stories for what they were--episodes meant to amuse and fascinate. She herself had often met doubters, especially small-minded bitches whose lives were so devoid of excitement that they could not appreciate truly fascinating aspects of another's life and had to denigrate. Tod was pacified only to the extent that he should have been more cautious before telling the Matterhorn story, should have scoped the listeners to beware of anyone who might penetrate the fabric of fiction. In short, Tod fretfully blamed himself as Risa pacified him.

In the future, he reminded himself and Risa, he should research with more care and not thoughtlessly engage in any story that popped into his head from the old days. He had, in fact, been thinking about a totally new adventure; suppose he and Risa had survived a ship sinking? Not as grandiose as Titanic, but one easily believable--a ferry boat between Hong Kong and Macao, for example. Look up the disaster for details, practice, then test it at a small gathering. What did Risa think? She sat quiet as he drove through the suburbs toward downtown and their high-rise river retreat where the world below seemed so malleable. How'd they escape from the ferry? Tod wasn't sure; they'd work it out. Yes, Risa said, smoking with thoughtless puffs while staring absently at the pewter moon glow on the river, let's see how far we can get with it.

LIFE MODELS

The Brattner's had the most irritating habit of dropping in whenever the mood struck them. Rosk was a portly, middle-aged ex-army captain, Sharilyn his wife more lean and wiry, and their four children, two boys and two girls ranged from eight to fifteen, were irrepressible. My wife and I had made the mistake of befriending them once or twice, after which they were attached to us with magnetic intensity. Have you ever tried to separate two large magnets? It can only be done by slipping them sideways till you have reduced surface contact enough to wrench them apart.

That's what we tried with the Brattner's: refusing invitations to visit them at their West St. Louis split-level, not answering our door when we noticed their Pontiac station wagon out front and, when caught unawares, making sudden excuses that they had caught us on our way out. These dodges worked most times, but not when they arrived and came around the side of the house and found the two of us lounging in lawn chairs beneath our elms and oaks. It was hard to mask our displeasure, but they took no notice or, if they did, said they had been passing by and only wanted to stay for a few minutes. That led to an impromptu meal and another miserable termination of our relaxed solitude.

The problem wasn't just their incessant presence; they were the most superficial and uninteresting people we had ever known. None of them had anything cogent to say on any subject. *The recent Arab-Israeli war?* Nothing. *Resulting gasoline shortage?* Huh uh. *Price controls?* Nope. *Watergate and President Nixon's impeachment?* Not a thought. All they did was blather--about food, children, school, yard work, needle point, clothing, shoes, car repairs, storm windows, screen doors, leaf-raking, fence mending, haircuts, cavities, eye glasses, carpet, drapes, and painting--both inside and outside versus wallpaper and aluminum siding.

We tried at first to accept their compulsive gregariousness as just one of the facts of nature encountered in the vast Midwest: wild tornadoes, golf ball-size hailstones on a humid spring afternoon, thunderstorms like dynamite detonations in the back yard, and icicle rain crackling onto the driveway like sheet metal splinters. The Brattner's were that, and more. It became impossible to get them out of mind even when they weren't in our company. They'd become atmospheric, a social deppressive force even when miles away. We often speculated, in morose moments, if they sat around blabbing till suddenly deciding to go visit someone.

There was no completely satisfying solution we could contemplate short of rudely telling them we didn't enjoy their company and would they please not drop by anymore. Civility kept us from doing that, and so we endured until my work provided a transfer to Seattle. We informed friends and neighbors with sincere regret, and the Brattner's with hardly disguised satisfaction. They broke their pattern of vacuity by expressing genuine sadness, and invited us to a farewell dinner at their house. We went, gratified that it'd be the last time we'd have to put up with them. The occasion was all that we expected--the same heavy pot roast, boiled potatoes, carrots and peas, and thickly-crusted peach pie cooling on the kitchen counter.

But there was one surprise--a couple we'd never met: Rosk's brother, Drake, his wife, Talia, and their son and daughter matched perfectly with the Brattner's eight and ten-year olds. Incestuous resemblance to the Brattner's was immediate--pink skin, ruddy blonde hair, merry emerald green eyes, and meaty lips that seemed to savor food before, during, and after they'd eaten. Following the meal, but before dessert, we learned this family earned a solid income modeling. What? Everything. They were photographic models, having appeared in numerous magazines and catalogs over several years. I must have acted skeptical, and Drake went out to his car, a Buick, and brought in their current portfolio. My wife and I sat on the couch as they turned pages to show us what they had been doing professionally for magazine advertisements, sales brochures and various catalogs.

There they were. Drake, Talia, sometimes with the children, in decorated living rooms, around a kitchen table, relaxing at poolside in a resort, or caught dining fashionably in a ritzy restaurant. I found myself looking from the lush photos of gracious, elegantly-attired beautiful people to the mundane, and quite plain folks beside us. The word 'photogenic' came to me; in person they were peasants, but pictorially aristocratic. A camera lens, appropriate light, makeup, wardrobe, and--ideal pictures of artistic value! It was the first time the contrast between naked reality and stylized imagery had come to my attention. As I looked and compared, and tried to listen carefully to what Drake and Talia were saying about specific posing events, they were lively, enthused and quite interesting. But, when they broke away for a family matter—they became as dull as the Brattners.

During coffee with peach pie and ice cream, I kept studying our social torturers--the Brattner's--wondering if they also possessed some of the photographic qualities of Rosk's brother. Table conversation was insufferable while I glanced around the dining room, living room and den, seeking Brattner photographs. Eventually I saw a portrait of Rosk and Sharilyn, he in army uniform and she in a puce chiffon formal, as if at a social event. He looked younger by two decades, bright-eyed, smiling, full of hope; she seemed shyness personified. The vacuity of their behavior is latent in the photograph: they are live-for-the-moment, unreflective people who will spend their entire lives without having or expressing any worthwhile thought. No lens would make them beautiful people.

My wife and I were quiet on the drive home Thoughts troubled my mind about truth versus falsehood, what was real and unreal. I caught flashing glimpses of her face as car beams highlighted it, leaving a residual image while I tried to focus on driving. Is she, am I, are we, photogenic in a truthful way? We are educated, articulate and active. Do photographs honestly depict our character? Are we *actual* in the chemical transfer images revealed to the objective lens? I drove frantically, anxious to return home and look at photos we haven't yet put in an album, our scrapbook of life.

Talk at the house turned casual. I wanted to find photos showing how vibrant we were, but had no desire to mention it to her. It seemed like a petty, trivial ambition, and wondered if she was considering it as well, resisting the urge to see ourselves as we are. She went to brush her teeth and ready for bed. I waited to join her. She was in bed, dozing. I nestled beside her, we clasped hands, an intimacy before sleep. Soon her breathing was soft, like the river breeze in the honeysuckle bushes near the window. An hour or two later I woke from doleful sleep, tumbled out of bed, and padded down to the desk where we kept our photos.

My heart thudded mournfully as I feared what was to come. There they were, an array of photos, taken in blissfully innocent poses on festive or placid occasions. I searched for some that displayed what I felt myself to be, but discovered only emptiness. I longed for images of depth; none. Plain as the Brattner's. We were leaving them, but *our* ordinariness would go with *us*.

OLDY & WEAKING

O utrage dominated the stolid face of the Chinese men's room attendant. What had begun as Travis's necessary visit to urinate in the steel trough lining one board wall of the men's room was spiraling into an international incident. The Chinese man was furious in his purple shirt and brown pants that seemed too short for his frame. Tan legs spindled below knees to bony ankles and scrawny feet encased in green plastic sandals. Waving both arms at Travis and wagging a finger at the camera lens, he shook his head and uttered Mandarin with such vehemence that it was clear Travis would get no photo of the toilet door and its ludicrous sign.

"What's his problem?" Mr. Drake asked Travis.

Travis glanced back at the portly Oregonian at the urinal who was shaking his penis before tucking it back into his yellow Bermuda shorts like a plump grub. The blue poplin hat bought in the gift shop of their Beijing hotel was canted at a rakish angle as Drake smiled at Travis's consternation over the fuss he'd provoked.

HUNCHING HOMEWARD

"It's that sign," Travis said, pointing at one of the white door stalls.

"What sign?" Drake said as he zipped himself up.

"I only wanted a photo because it's so funny."

"What's it mean?" Drake hiked his shorts above his gut. "Doesn't make sense."

Travis felt equally portly, the overfed American in a nation of slight people who ate at lightning speed with chopsticks. He studied the door to be sure that what had made him laugh and take out his camera was real. Painted on the white stall door was a sign in red letters so garish that it made him chuckle even confronting the strident Chinese man.

FUR SPECIALY USE
OLDY & WEAKING

"I think it's for the disabled or elderly," Travis said, lowering his camera to pacify the Chinese man's effort to avoid his taking a photo. "If I'd thought he'd go ballistic--"

"Hell," Drake said, "it cost a Yuan to get in here. The least he could do is let you amuse yourself while having a piss."

"Sorry," Travis said to the Chinese man. "Just a quick picture."

He lofted his camera and gestured toward the toilet stall door.

"No, no, no!" the man shrieked and waved both arms.

"Holy good goddamn," Drake said.

Travis was stunned. "What the hell's he so upset about?"

"Does he think you're going to steal his soul?" Drake quipped.

"What?" Travis didn't know what Drake was talking about.

"You know, natives who think the camera takes the soul."

"You think he has his soul behind the toilet stall door?"

Drake shrugged. "Maybe if you give him another coin."

"What for?" Travis didn't want to admit that his initial amusement when he saw the sign was dissipated by the dispute. "I gave the old lady outside a Yuan to get in here."

"Baksheesh maybe," Drake said. "In countries like this, running a men's room is a profitable family business enterprise."

Travis tried to decide how much it mattered to have a photo of the admonition. It was an impulse, induced by the hilarity of seeing the mangled syntax. Ever since arriving in Beijing the day before and touring the Forbidden City and Ming Dynasty Tombs, he'd taken it for granted that he could photograph whatever he chose. The humorous signage in the deepest tomb, with words broken in mid-syllable at the end of each line, set him up for this incident. It was the only levity after that descent down narrow steps into the bowels of the labyrinth squeezed between bustling tourists. He felt trapped and suffocated by animal closeness, but stayed calm only by holding his breath in the intoxicating air fetid with exhaled garlic and ginger.

Since photos were prohibited in the tomb, he agreed with Drake that he should be able to snap something truly memorable, like the damned toilet stall sign. It was so ridiculous to make a fuss over nothing. He searched for another Yuan coin, those exotic copper charms that produced both smiles and upraised palms. It was worth it to quiet the crazed man, take the damned picture, and lam out of there and back onto the tour bus. The man refused the coin and attempted to push Travis out of the men's room.

"Hey, dammit!" Travis said, jerking himself back and away.

"Go, you go, go," the man squealed, pushing Travis to leave.

"Insistent bastard," Drake said as he finished rinsing his hands at the sink with a running faucet of amber-colored water and snatched a thin paper towel. "Somebody's on the verge of losing face, if the Commies still permit such behavior."

"Not me, dammit," Travis said, flipping the Yuan coin at the petulant man.

It bounced onto the concrete floor and spun a few times before settling, like a temple offering, near a grated water drain. The odors of urine and pungent disinfectant, along with the surgical sensation that he was in an alien country, suddenly assailed him. It was a disheartening reminder of how compressed and vulnerable he'd felt in the depths of the tomb crushed between Chinese bodies in the morbid half darkness of what seemed like a mass burial among strangers--a sense of mortality in an uncaring universe.

"Go on, take it." He glared at the Chinese man. "That's for one lousy photo."

Before he could ready his camera again, the old man shouted out the door. The chunky, middle-aged woman who had collected coins from men on their way into the restroom, shuffled in with a wide-eyed expression. Furious grunts ensued. The woman shook her head at Travis. The Chinese man folded his arms as the woman took over.

"Must be his old lady," Drake laughed off to the side. "Let's get our butts out of this place, Travis, before I have to pee again and pony up another coin."

"All I wanted was a stupid picture," Travis said, stomach churning as he realized he hadn't even used the urinal yet, the sign having caught his eye and diverted him away from his renal task. He hung the camera on his shoulder by its strap and indicated that he wanted to use the toilet. "Is it okay?" he said to the man, ignoring the woman. He eased toward the door of the signed stall. "Potty time--okay?"

Before he could grasp the brass handle and open the door, both the man and the woman began shouting. Travis got no more than a quick peek inside at a porcelain toilet and paper roll. There was nothing to mark it as especially for anybody aged or feeble. He laughed as he realized the only thing worth noting was the sign itself on the door. Before he could retreat to the urinal, he found that the woman had gone out and come back with a policeman in a coffee-colored uniform; the man wasn't armed, but had a stick hanging from his shiny black leather belt and looked menacing nonetheless as only an impassive Oriental face can. It didn't seem proper at that moment to expose his organ at the urinal, so Travis decided to remain silent and wait for somebody to say something.

"I'll get the tour guide," Drake said, slipping outside in a subdued manner.

"What you want?" the policeman asked Travis, stern despite his youth.

"I want to relieve myself," Travis said, pointing toward the urinal.

"Uh," the policeman uttered, perplexed.

"I came in to pee," Travis said as he put the camera in its case.

The policeman addressed the man. They talked for a few seconds, the policeman turning to glance at Travis several times when the man pointed toward him, then had to listen as the woman began jabbering and gesturing toward Travis. When the policeman appeared to have heard enough, he turned to Travis while the woman glowered and kept her lips in motion as though issuing muted threats that didn't require sound.

The policeman said, "You one time insult this man?"

Travis sucked a deep breath. "I only wanted a picture."

"Piksha?"

"Of that stall door."

The policeman turned toward the stall, studied it curiously, and then stared back at Travis with a puzzled expression. "Why want you piksha?"

His bladder seemed full to bursting at this instant, but Travis had decided on conciliation, anything that might restore the world to calm and permit a satisfying pee before getting on the bus. Tourists paraded in and out of the restroom in an endless array of urinary relief. If he only could join them, become as anonymous as before and immerse himself in toilet routine.

"It was so striking, unusual," he said, adding, "a considerate sign meant to help elderly or disabled people. I thought friends in America would like to see it."

"Uh humm," the policeman said. He spoke to the man, and then to Travis once again with the hint of a smile. "Okay, take piksha. Two Yuan."

"One's over there on the floor," Travis said, "and I don't have any more coins."

As much as he wanted to take the picture, piss, and get out of there, paying again for the privilege seemed like abjectly surrendering a principle. Drake came in behind Mr. Ling, the tour guide, a spry man in a black suit and tie with shiny gray hair, merry eyes, and a thin moustache. He began chatting with the policeman, noted the man and woman, nodded several times while Travis received sly glances and winks from Drake, and then he faced Travis and led him a few paces aside by one arm.

"Ah, Mr. Travis, sir. Some difficulty. Old man think you spy with camera, try get him in difficulties with government authorities."

"For god's sakes, I only wanted a photo of that silly door."

"Yes, yes--understand. Is best we should go now."

"I haven't even had a chance to pee yet."

"Ah--get to bus and we make stop after ten minutes."

"I already paid a Yuan to get in here, and tossed another coin...."

Two soldiers came in, small automatic rifles on their shoulders. They gave an immediate impression of absolute authority because even the policeman was humbled and the old man and woman backed away. Pee or not, Travis was ready to leave. No one spoke. The soldiers studied each of them as if trying to decide who they expected to escort from the room. It was Mr. Ling who explained in Mandarin whatever it was that needed explanation. Without changing their stony expression or any indication of acceptance, the soldiers eyed each of them for endless seconds before leaving with the indifference of armed men among creatures helpless in their presence. Mr. Ling spoke to the man and woman, gave them a five Yuan note, and ushered Travis and Drake outside.

"You shouldn't have done that," Travis told him, irritated that he now felt further indebted to Mr. Ling. "I already tried to pay him."

"It a small matter," Mr. Ling said, urging him and Drake toward the bus.

"Why all the goddamned fuss over a simple photograph?" Drake said.

"Country people own toilet, have pride, most anxious of trouble."

"What kind of trouble?" Travis said, uneasy that it was his fault.

"Some people very fearsome," Mr. Ling said.

"Fearsome?" Travis said. "You mean afraid?"

"Ah, yes, sorry. Afraid of some bad troubles."

"What the hell are they scared of?" Drake said.

"Nothing," Mr. Ling said. "We get to bus quick."

Drake whispered to Travis, "Paranoid bastards."

Travis had forgotten how humid and hot the afternoon was. Tourists bustled by the food stands around the parking

HUNCHING HOMEWARD

lot. Mr. Ling walked alongside on stumpy legs toward their bus, which idled with its door open, air conditioner blasting. Gray-haired women stared at him through the tinted windows, imperious eyes blaming Travis for their delayed departure while hundreds of Chinese shuffled past him humble and cautious. He glimpsed himself in the window next to the door before climbing into the bus--an elderly widower who had behaved badly. Wending up the narrow aisle, rheumy eyes examining him, he dreaded Mr. Ling's promise to stop so he could urinate. Oldy and weaking for sure; he'd rather do penance with a bloated bladder.

CLIMBING MT. TI'EN

Stepping off the air-conditioned tour bus that humid May afternoon provided Reid with a full tourist's-eye view of the awesome mini-mountain. It jutted from the flood plain of the Li River near Guilin with the etherealness of cloud-shrouded peaks depicted in scrolls from the Ming Dynasty. Slate gray granite soared like an upended breadloaf. Reid studied its carved steps and protective iron rails. Tour members descended the bus, men with cameras, the wives clutching handbags while juggling water bottles. There were seven widows; he was the widower, seated during meals with one or more available ladies.

"Stay somehow, please," the guide, Miss Liang cooed, bustling in her beige skirt and white cotton blouse as if she could keep them apart from other tourists crowding the pavement by the entrance. "Keep here so much I am get tickets."

Reid disliked crowds but accepted the press of humanity when visiting populous places. The group provided a buffer of compatriots. One or more of the 'Widows Club' remained near him. Thin or stout, white-haired or dyed, they displayed flirty deference. Having survived one wife, a fine women in her way, he remained uneasy while enduring old age with careful travel and the occasional joys of his children and grandchildren. It was, however, unsettling to confront anxieties he had long ago identified as spiritual or philosophical, and discarded in his youth.

He gazed upward at Mt. Ti'en as Miss Liang guided them through the entrance to the first steps. She stopped under plum trees adorned with chattering birds. Reid wiped moisture from his face and neck in the shade, the poplin hat sweatband cool against his forehead. The clammy short sleeve shirt sluiced shivers through him. Addie Willis idled nearby him as Miss Liang discoursed about the mountain.

Despite the difficulty hearing amid Chinese babble and birds overhead, which led Reid to speculate that maybe the birds chirped in Mandarin, he was able to pick up Miss Liang's spiel: *The historical important of mountain named for Chinese word Heaven, a pilgrimage of monks and devouts to climb thousand years because summit bring peace. The 333 steps to top, a divine number to explore life and death, and eternalness.*

Eternalness. A mere word, but it left Miss Liang's rosette lips and lingered in the mind despite Reid's concern about the steep climb as she went on to explain that it would take about an hour, and if some did not feel up to it, they might remain, or climb part way and then come back down. Everyone seemed game to try, so Reid took a deep breath and shuffled ahead after three widows with the remaining four behind, Addie Willis just behind him. He looked at her when she mumbled, her bright green eyes in a wrinkled, but not unpleasant, face.

"Oh, sorry, Mr. Bentley," she said. "Only encouraging myself."

"I thought maybe you wished to go ahead of me," Reid said.

"Good heavens, no," she chuckled, "unless you agree to push."

"You may have to shove me," he said, glancing at the rump of the lady ahead in blue gabardine Bermuda shorts. The notion of Addie Willis placing her hands on his backside was ludicrous as the first crush of effort hit after a dozen steps. "It's occurred to me," he muttered, "that the only view for a while will be rear ends."

Addie Willis laughed, but the lady just ahead, usually smiles and pleasantries, glowered pink-faced. It humbled him and he focused on one step at a time, pacing his breathing, fearing weakness with the monumental climb before reaching the summit. It surprised him that he'd resolved to climb all the way. He walked at home every day, exercised for fitness, and was in good shape for his age, but not full of stamina. Each step, ten inches high, was carved from the granite of Mt. Ti'en. After the first hundred, climbers paused to rest. Reid sucked air, noting how high they were above the parking lot, trees, and tile rooftops of the rustic village.

He clutched the iron rail as he looked down. It was a sensation unlike any he had sensed before. Riding outside elevators up the side of buildings, or watching from high-rise windows, didn't produce the same lightheaded-ness. Here he felt the humid breeze against his sweaty face, smelled smoke from charcoal fires and the aroma of ginger and pepper wafting from cook pots where vendors stir-fried pungent snacks. He recalled a sawdust smell and swarthy dankness of farmers' overalls and lilac water scent from their wives as revivalists clapped and sang in a tent on the Dakota prairie. On Mt. Ti'en the strongest odor was his maleness amidst cedar clumps in the granite crevices.

Addie prodded to remind him the climbers were ascending. His legs had become lead weights, the athletic shoes swampy anchors on each foot. He wiped sweat from his face as his heavy breathing was accented by gasps from the lady ahead and Addie behind. The jokes that had earlier punctuated the effort dwindled to a 'Dammit' from one of the husbands or 'Gracious' from a wife or widow. Reid was almost spent when they stopped and he was able to gaze at the rice paddy countryside and peaks adorned with pine and cedar along the Li River.

It reminded him of his life-long struggle to believe and doubts about a Superior Being who watched over mankind. He'd decided that despite such grandeur, the world merely *existed*, was here when he arrived, and would persist in a natural state after his departure. Addie seized an opportunity to sit, so he squatted, staring at the curl of her gray-brown hair and soft swirl of both ears. *Meat flowers,* he thought, smiling at the absurd reference--weird appendages, fleshy curlicues--to corral human sounds and unearthly din.

As the tour above him resumed moving, he ached trying to stand. It was like the first time he'd attended Catholic Mass while in Japan with the army. They had been ordered into Korea, a combat zone, and with fervor, soldiers who'd gotten drunk and whored, felt a need to atone and prepare for possible oblivion. Reid attended out of curiosity, with his buddy, Raul Garcia, who said during the service that so many Protestants had shown up there was no room for Catholics. Sitting, standing, kneeling and Latin fascinated Reid, inducing naive submission to some higher power whether his brain accepted or not.

He climbed upward, choking and weary till, with a burst of coarse energy, he got to the summit. They stood twitching and breathless on the platform behind the waist-high metal rail. Buddhist monks in saffron robes stood with hands clasped while they chanted. He gazed about at the mountain peaks dominating the verdant landscape of paddies, huts, cedar groves, and along the riverbank, water buffalo grazing in stolid antiquity as if captured in a pastoral silkscreen.

Despite every rational impulse, he was enthralled. Perhaps there was something to that other part of human existence after all. There must be more to life than the stale cynicism of the cerebral cortex and longing for closure that led mankind to create godliness. Cameras clicked, wives and widows exclaimed. Addie, standing alongside, didn't aim her camera or behave like a tourist. She gazed at the splendor as though silence was the only devout reaction. After striding the summit as a twosome, she looked at him with a quizzical expression, the lines splayed at the corners of her eyes tightly crinkled.

"I suppose we should take a photo," she said, but made no move to remove her camera from its case. "Seems the thing to do."

"Uh, huh," Reid said, not taking out his camera either, then adding. "On the other hand, it might be more memorable to save it in the mind's eye."

The phrase sounded trivial. What was the mind's eye, or the heart of hearts, such inane *cliches*? Was he so thrilled by the sublime view that he felt compelled to triteness? Addie smiled in apparent sympathy and remained silent while appreciating the sight. He noted that the group had become strangely quiet after their initial outburst of enthusiasm. No sarcasm when they'd clambered up earlier hillsides to visit Buddhist temples with garish statues. This site made even hard hearts tender and worth savoring for its own sake.

Then it was time to start back, clinging to the inside rail as they stepped out into space and downward. Suddenly, he recalled--it was while descending the spiral stairs in the Statue of Liberty--it would be painful, sore legs required to ease downward with caution, straining weary muscle tissues. Reid felt the first agonizing twinge after only going fifty steps, glancing at the strained faces of upward climbers passing on his left. Why hadn't he noticed on the way up, the anguish on every face descending? The pain was so intense the men and women in his group laughed and groaned, before uttering the cruel truth that what goes up must come down.

It thrust his brain backward to descending a hemp net over the side of a troopship in Inchon Harbor, both hands grasping cross ropes in the mesh already damp and slippery from previous soldiers as he wondered if he should switch and clutch the vertical strands that might be drier. His arms and legs quivered with effort and fear, thinking he'd tumble and land in the LCT, or break his back on its edge before plunging into the water between it and the ship to drown or be crushed to death. He hung paralyzed in total dread, unable to move, strength slipping from his fingers, quaking feet encased in combat boots. Just as he felt he would fall, a strong hand grabbed one pack strap. The huge Negro sergeant held him, and then stayed alongside as Reid eased the rest of the way till his feet hit the rolling LCT deck. Salvation--a guardian angel!

His panic was so intense he forgot he was going down stone steps. There seemed no stopping as the line of bodies kept cascading downward like a throng of crazed animals. He felt himself start to lose balance, like a man on a steep slope who descends slowly at first, careful to keep control, then faster till he's rushing downhill unable to keep his legs out front and knowing that in seconds he'll be in a free fall. A hand gripped his left shoulder hard. He grabbed the steel rail with both hands and steadied himself.

The woman in front continued to move lower but he stood without attempting the next step. The hand was hot. He turned and saw Addie, her cheeks flushed, eyes somber. Her lips moved in breathless spasms, but he heard nothing. She hadn't tried to keep him from pitching forward, but to steady herself. That explained the pressure he'd reacted to. After a few seconds, she smiled and soundlessly mouthed, 'Sorry.'

He was engulfed by her presence, the pulsating animal-ness of the human body, the locus of the cancer that had devoured his wife: the wan face, weary with struggle, pleading for release, praying with the fervor of her Lutheran upbringing for the god of gods, deliverer of mercy, to receive her immortal soul to its bosom. Reid mumbled religious platitudes, empathized with all his love, and knew with each passing day and night that he was embroiled in a charade, unable to comfort with soul-satisfying conviction since he was adrift in a remorseless universe. Her pastor consoled as Reid damned the blind fate that inflicted such torture on a human being.

In the end she had gone in her sleep while he sat holding a withered hand. He had been roused by the hospice nurse. As much as he desired to release his grip on that basket of skin and bones, he felt viscerally duty bound to cradle it longer than any comfort he might convey. At last, the nurse had hugged his shoulders and gently removed his hand from the dead fingers, placing his wife's cool arm under a pale blanket, and then waited as Reid planted a dry kiss on his wife's forehead before covering the body and leaving him with the image of mounds and curves under snow-covered foothills. Spirit had left her body, and the body left his life, wheeled away down a twilight hospital hall.

He patted Addie's hand pressed against his cheek, felt the wetness streaming from both eyes, then clasped it firmly in his right hand while grasping the iron rail in his left. He uttered something about it being okay, did she feel ready to keep going? She took a deep breath and nodded. They neared the base of Mt. Ti'en; its gray eminence loomed above them. When they got down to linger in the midst of the breathless, relieved group, Miss Liang weaved through them with bottles of water and a benevolent smile, chatting amiably. As the group regained normal breathing and composure, they praised the profound experience.

Reid stood among them, unconcerned about crowding or his bare arm brushing anyone else as they chattered and reached out to one another. He held the water bottle Miss Liang had given him in his left hand, not sure why he hadn't opened it to drink. His right hand still held Addie's left hand, warm and moist in his as she held her bottle in her right hand. They gazed at each other, realized they were still holding hands like infatuated teenagers, grinned, let go, and gulped water greedily. Reid didn't feel spiritual, merely peaceful. On the bus, it seemed natural to sit with Addie Willis during the ride to their Guilin hotel.

A PALACE INCIDENT

When Andrew Eccleston went missing from our Yangtze cruise ship the night before Wuhan, my first thought was, "He swam to infinity after all." It was an odd idea, but most of the travelers considered the wiry old timer a peculiar duck, although a few concluded that he was cranky and crazy as a loon. They were accurate about Andrew's acerbic demeanor, thin-lipped with sunken gray eyes, and eccentric. He delivered cynical remarks to our guide in Tianamen Square and the Forbidden City in Beijing, and called ghostly 'Halloos' when we were deep into one of the Ming Dynasty Tombs. Then there was his childishness at the Summer Palace.

Nobody on the tour sought to know him very well once they found out he had a caustic attitude about every aspect of the three-week trip to China. Why he ventured it was odd. At first as a single man, like myself, wifeless due to time and mortality, we received polite attentiveness from the widows. I accepted it while gently deflecting the most matronly flirtations. But after his behavior at the palace, no widow courted him.

It took a while to discern his main gripe with the world: He had, with diligence, played by the rules and retired in a sprawling Los Angeles suburb. After navy service in World War II, he turned his interest in machines toward work as a mechanic in an aircraft plant. He liked to transform steel ingots or sheet aluminum into useful objects the world admired. After retiring he was idle and hobby-less beyond viewing television. When his wife died following a savage battle with cancer, he found himself sitting alone in the bungalow until persuaded to take this trip.

His attitude toward the historical grandeur and opulence we were witnessing in China oscillated between morose comments about how many toilets an emperor would need to the sardonic observation that thousands of miserable slaves had built the palaces and tombs for a few rotten royals. The world, he griped, consisted of givers and takers, and the takers were bastards. I'd seen pyramids in Egypt and Yucatan and agreed with him. But I also believed that mankind had improved and we might look ahead, despite lapses, to a better future for *homo sapiens*.

I was the only one who'd sit with him on the bus or tolerate his diatribes. When I gave him my viewpoint on things, he looked at me as if I had either spent most of my life protected from the harsh realities of life or become a witless optimist. As he lamented the unfairness of life and what it was like to watch somebody writhe in cancerous agony, it irritated me. Although my wife had passed in comparative peace with her weak heart, I carried grief just as he did and was loathe to offer any more sympathy than he deserved. When I ignored him, he shut down; it was temporary till something else set him off.

While we toured the luxurious Summer Palace halls, gardens, bridges, courtyards, lakes, temples and floral-festooned walks, Andrew went berserk. It represented the labor of slaves, but it was possible to admire its beauty despite so much suffering. The palace seemed a metaphor for life: from agony and toil comes splendor. Even the Great Wall, a monument to misery, was quite a majestic wonder surpassing its brutal creation.

When the tour reached the man-made lake with the multi-arched bridge reflected across the water like a granite necklace, we came to ostentation gone awry: the Marble Boat built into the lake. In it the Dowager Empress had often meandered with her court ladies to contemplate the beauties of nature as they sipped tea or smoked opium. Andrew griped about imperial sloth. The stone ramp that would have allowed us to walk onto the Marble Boat and enjoy its splendid scenic view of the lake, bridge and palace, was roped off to visitors. After photos, we were led toward a courtyard. Chinese voices began chattering. We saw Andrew climb over the rope and walk to the Marble Boat, striding with gangly legs and slight torso like a Mandarin. The guide called to him. I watched Andrew in his Bermuda shorts and sport shirt till he stood at the prow. I'm not sure he had any more in mind than defying authority to stand where no peasants were allowed. The idea that it was a rehearsal for a more serious escapade later crossed my mind, but that would have required concluding that what Andrew finally did was calculated rather than impulsive. The guide kept calling him in her bird-like voice to 'Come quick back!' and 'Not go such!' and "Hurry or most difficult!'

The group chuckled at Andrew's childish prank and the guide's pathetic effort. As she scampered to the boat ramp, two khaki-uniformed men began running along the stone walkway bordering the lake, jabbering in Chinese as they pointed at Andrew. He stood in utter calm, his arms across his chest, staring across the rippling water at the arched bridge. When he turned toward the tumult behind and saw the guards approaching, he smiled before facing the lake. He dove into the water without posing, an awkward splash that for all its inelegance struck me as graceful, maybe because it barely disturbed the pristine serenity of the view.

The sharp cries of our tour guide were accented by harsh shouts from the guards who ran to the prow of the boat and waved at the receding swimmer. He surged ahead like a flailing child into the breeze-swept lake. I thought I heard him singing with each stroke, his plastic-sandaled feet slapping the ochre water in his wake. The group, like a suddenly curious gaggle of obedient school children, gathered at the ramp and called to him. Some husbands snapped photos or video taped the bizarre event.

The guide, flush-faced and dabbing at perspiration, assembled us in the shade, mumbling 'Very bad' till she had to explain to other men in uniform and then hustle us into a courtyard. I noticed a small boat speed toward ever-remote Andrew. It was during those timeless minutes that I considered the depth of the lake. Was it possible for a man to stand in the middle? Did Andrew mean to swim to the arched bridge or sink beneath the surface? The motorboat with its crew of three guards caught the now hapless man and, after several futile attempts to grab and haul him aboard, managed to drag his body from the water like a cadaver.

The rest of the tour was overshadowed by the mishap. The women offered apologies to the guide, who did her best to act as though nothing untoward had happened. When we returned to our bus, the door stood open, two rigid guards waiting. As we boarded I looked for Andrew, wondering if he was under arrest and we'd never see him again. I made my way to the back and saw his body stretched across the back seat. It struck me that he'd drowned, and the Chinese, not sure what to do, had merely laid him out in the back of the bus like a corpse that smelled of mold and sweat. Andrew raised himself, yawned, grinned, and stared at us passengers in the aisle, and then scooted to the window where he gazed into the late afternoon sun.

It would be an exaggeration to say that he became the group's pariah, but nobody went out of their way to speak with him or even acknowledge his presence with a nod or smile, the least civility that would have been accorded any ordinary human being. Even I hesitated to be sociable, but after Xian, Chunqing, and boarding the cruise ship, I stood beside him at the rail silently watching the river bank, peasants in rice paddies, and children tending cattle or goats.

So far as I know, during meals or the several dockings and shore-side trips into river towns or sampan excursions up tributaries, Andrew was never addressed, or tried to talk with anyone. He did eavesdrop near other passengers while cruising the river, but was subdued and mute. While observing the terra cotta army guarding the emperor's tomb in Xian, he remarked about the inanity of being one man in a world of billions who had lived and died, with billions more to come, a horde without hope.

We went to a museum to view the lifelike remains of a three-thousand-year-old man. I stared at the eerie countenance floating in pale blue fluid that seemed like gelatin, and became breathless as I gazed at Andrew with an expression so forlorn that it struck me as death-in-life. It made me contemplate the face of the ancient Chinese man in his liquid grave. The only dead face I'd ever seen was my wife's, in the hospital, her pale pink features cloaked in deathly sleep as if taking a short nap. The dead man with ghastly green eye sockets, drawn cheeks, and a mouth stretched tight, exemplified the sadness of having died and also the futility of life itself. Andrew might be that mummy glaring in gelatinous remorse.

It was a morbid reflection that lingered after Andrew's disappearance. He must have gone over the side at night. After the guide's report, we knew what had occurred. Talk was hushed. I gulped despair. I had hoped to avoid primal mortality on a grief-free trip. Instead, I'd witnessed a despondent man's rebellion against fate with his contemptuous plunge into time. I made an extra effort to mingle for the rest of the tour in order to keep life, such as it was, close at hand.

SITTING ROOM ONLY

As the tour bus left London on an early June morning, it was only two passengers over half-filled at twenty-six. Before reaching Plymouth in late afternoon, Mrs. Blount had asserted herself. Not content with room for each person to sit where they pleased, she decided it would be better if people rotated sides and front-back so the choicest seats for viewing were equitably distributed. Nobody minded till it became clear when the tourists stumbled sleepily aboard the next morning that, without specific seating arrangements it would be a frustrating jumble they had to sort out.

"Everybody, attention!" Mrs. Blount said. "The best approach is to seat yourself where you didn't sit yesterday, and so forth." That didn't clarify matters, so she added, "Come now, rotate," and sat beside her husband, who she'd guided to a window seat.

"What nonsense!" Emil Guthrie said. He wore a tan jumpsuit with a poplin hat, the kind often festooned with fishing flies. While struggling to put his daypack in the overhead rack, he muttered 'Nonsense,' for emphasis and scratched his beard. "Or," he continued, "as they say in Jolly Old England, Balderdash!"

"It's not at all," Mrs. Blount countered with a fierce glance before turning to her husband planted next to the window in the seat behind the driver.

She brushed at her red-gray curls as if to rearrange them, while her husband sat oblivious. As we'd learned at supper the night before, although he could see light and dark hues and overall shapes, he was legally blind and dependent on her. He gazed through the enormous windshield at nothing more picturesque than asphalt paving and nearby brick buildings. He was a long-faced man with a child-like demeanor toward Mrs. Blount and irritable if anyone else other than his wife tried to assist him.

She appealed her case to him with, "It's not nonsense at all, is it, Wendell?"

"Whatever you say, dear," Mr. Blount replied with dry, brittle agitation.

"And I say," Emil Guthrie quipped, "poppycock, bollocks, and bugger."

"We can all do without such coarse language," Mrs. Blount replied.

The passengers, variously assorted elder couples and singles, settled in seats with empty spaces between most. Mrs. Blount twisted about to see where everybody had put themselves and appeared displeased when the tour director, Mr. Pettibone, got aboard, counted his charges, and seated himself across from Brady, his brawny driver. Brady, a taciturn chap with flat black hair, started the engine and eased from the hotel parking lot. Before the bus had traveled a mile, Mrs. Blount leaned toward Mr. Pettibone expounding an earful of 'oughts' and 'shoulds'.

He nodded, his eyes glazed, mumbled an occasional comment, and grimaced as he grasped the microphone to address the group. After a cheerful 'Good morning,' and brief rundown of the day's itinerary, he concluded with a sermon about seating. There is, he said, plenty of room to move about; therefore it wouldn't be strictly necessary for the usual rotation of passengers that gave everyone an equal chance at the best sightseeing locations. So, in the spirit of cooperation and felicitous companionship, would everybody please be gracious about seating accommodations? A sighing assent was exhaled by the group as though a great weight had been lifted from their collective shoulders. Emil Guthrie acclaimed, 'Hear, hear!' to applause. Only Mrs. Blount seemed to be displeased. She slouched into her seat and stared ahead.

By custom, the seat one took each morning should've been the one occupied the balance of the day. But, as if to flaunt the fair-minded nature of Mr. Pettibone's request, Mrs. Blount seated herself and her husband in various seats, moving about randomly front to back, right to left, till nobody was sure where they'd settle. Mr. Pettibone joked at first, and then shrugged as she performed her weird version of musical chairs.

It was left to Emil Guthrie to make it an issue. During lunch stops, where the meal was served in a group dining room, he sat first in one chair, then another, asking one or two others if they were satisfied with their place at the table. It became a game for two or three men to pretend they wanted to move and make a grandiose fuss. During the charade, Mrs. Blount stayed where she sat with her husband and maintained a look of chilly disdain. For several mornings thereafter she sat in the choice seat behind Brady. In the interest of comity for the tour of England, Wales, Ireland and Scotland, Mr. Pettibone relented. Emil Guthrie, however, did not concede defeat.

One morning in Wales, as everyone boarded, the entire group sat on the right side behind Mrs. and Mr. Blount, and remained the entire day leaving the left side empty. The next morning, half sat behind while the other twelve filled the left front side opposite the Blounts, leaving the back half empty. During the day they shifted seats with one another, laughing and joking. Mrs. Blount became a lump of hostility while Mr. Blount, troubled by what was happening, seemed helpless to do anything but sit where his wife prescribed. In Dublin, Emil Guthrie and a large single woman with an infectious laugh and merry face boarded first and staked their claim to the two seats behind Brady.

"What is this?" Mrs. Blount demanded, confronting Emil Guthrie and holding up tour members lined up in the hotel parking lot. "Just what do you think you're going?"

"And what is it you're about this morning, darling?" Emil Guthrie said in a mock-Irish brogue so thick it lingered in the air like a pungent fog that made Mrs. Blount blink and lurch backward. "Is it an uproar you'll be giving us?"

Behind Mrs. Blount stood Mr. Blount, a step or two below, anxious to climb into the bus. He nudged her several times and mumbled something that made her tremble as if shaking off a swarm of bees. She turned about and glared.

"Not now, dear! I'm trying to settle something serious up here."

"Settle it later," he said, giving her a shove. "People want to board, *dear*!"

"Wendell," she said, bile edging her tone. "They've taken *our* seats."

"Not at all," Emil Guthrie said. "We're simply *rotating* ourselves."

"You're trying to provoke me. I won't stand for such boorishness."

"Delilah!" Mr. Blount said, more of a growl than an utterance. "Shut up and find other seats!" In the shocked silence that ensued he added, "For God's sakes!"

"Faith and begorra!" Emil Guthrie said with glee. "She's a Delilah. And sure that says all there is to know. She'll be giving us emasculating haircuts soon enough."

Mrs. Blount seemed to shrivel before Emil Guthrie. Brady smiled a pub leer as if well into his cups and covered his mouth as he chuckled. Mr. Pettibone's voice could be heard outside asking what was holding up things. With another shove from Mr. Blount, she scrambled into the aisle and went to the back of the bus, where she stood as if not sure about sitting. After a moment of indecision, she clutched her shoulder bag and sat down next to the right side window. Mr. Blount sat, leaving a couple spaces between them. The tour group noticed Mrs. Blount remotely situated in the rear and commented cheerily that yet another seating scheme was undergoing trial-and-error.

During that particular day's travel and touring, Mrs. Blount remained in the back of the bus, sometimes not getting off for even brief visits or bathroom breaks, but when she did, always returning to her self-imposed isolation. The next day, and for those that followed, she led an increasingly reluctant Mr. Blount to the same area. And then, much to everyone's surprise, he settled himself midway on the left side of the bus, next to the window although everyone understood that he wouldn't be able to view what was passing with any clarity. In the middle of that day's touring, Emil Guthrie placed himself beside Mr. Blount. Now and then he described a pastoral scene or quaint village they motored through. Mrs. Blount remained in back while other passengers arrayed themselves about the coach amid new friendships and conviviality much to Mr. Pettibone's satisfaction.

For another week or so, after the tour crossed from Ireland back into Wales and worked up the west coast toward Scotland, Mrs. Blount maintained her vigil in the back of the bus. Emil Guthrie often found himself assisting Mr.

Blount when his wife did not rush to do so, but the couple sat together during the dinners, talking in clipped phrases but without anger. When she boarded one drizzly morning and asked Mr. Blount where he'd like to sit, he turned toward her in astonishment, his usual plain expression graced with curiosity. He chose a seat toward the front, but not conspicuously so, and that tour day was comparatively uneventful and therefore pleasant.

Sometimes in the days following, Emil Guthrie sat close enough to chat with Mr. Blount. With the passage of languid time and lengthy miles, even Mrs. Blount became cordial and began to enjoy the final days of the tour. Seated near her husband in a more relaxed posture than before, she appeared to be more thoroughly *with* her husband than *in charge of* him, and when she and Emil Guthrie were seen sharing a laugh at the final dinner in London, the group enthusiastically celebrated the most unexpected outcome of the entire tour.

TOOTHLESS OLD MAN

The stick-like old man with one snaggle tooth loomed out of the morning fog toward Burl and left a lingering image of Middle Eastern peasant decay as he was passed. Burl gasped at the edge of his endurance but jogged on with every pound of his being. The orange designer running suit stretched taut over his hips and thighs. It was streaked with sweat despite the cool air. He sucked his paunch in as he paced by the pine-shaded roadway beside the country club, but that curtailed his wind and he let the gut sag back out like yeasted bread dough seeking space.

"Goddamned doctors!" he grunted in cadence with his thudding footfalls.

Burl relived the tedious physical the company required for insurance. He had frustrated attempts to get a complete checkup for years. He was a big man, ex-football player in college, appeared fit in vested suits, and spoke with a booming voice that proclaimed power and virility. But on that treadmill, plugged into a computer and respirator like a laboratory rat, the truth had emerged. It began at a fast walk.

The therapist announced each change of speed and angle of the rolling walkway. He ran to keep pace with the machine-groaning, sweating, straining. His legs decayed to lead; the room spun. He'd been on the damned thing long enough. He signaled to stop. His rubbery knees gave way and he wobbled nearly passing out.

"Damned embarrassing!" he exhaled as he turned up a meandering slope on the far side of the golf course.

"Mr. Hardy," the doctor'd said two weeks later, "you're fifty with the heart and lungs of a seventy-year-old."

Burl was outraged. "What the hell do you mean?"

"You're overweight and under-exercised. You smoke and drink excessively. Cholesterol level is three fifty plus."

"I'm a big man," Burl said in his defense. "I eat what I like and burn it off. I've smoked and drank for years without damage."

"No, you haven't," said the doctor. "You're on the brink: shortness of breath, irregular heart rhythm, poor oxygen use. If you don't change your lifestyle, at best you'll be uninsurable. At worst, you'll die."

Burl had gritted so hard then that he nearly dislodged his partial upper plate. He had to flex his tongue to shove it back; when it was out he looked…old.

"What do I have to do," Burl asked, fearfully humbled.

That was six months ago. Now he struggled along the roadway on a Sunday morning with his muscles screaming for rest. In the first weeks he'd cut out snacks and fatty entrees. But attending sales conventions and entertaining made it difficult. So he slacked off, then binged, jogged, dieted, and binged until it became a failing effort. When he quit cigarettes, he gained weight. When dieting, he got jittery and smoked. Jogging, he got too exhausted for anything.

"Bullshit!" he yelled. The sun burned through the misty morning.

Maybel had been more sympathetic than usual. She cooked lean foods, often walked alongside while he ran. But it didn't help. He was his own man, always had been. His job was to take care of her by being the dutiful provider.

When he completed the first one-mile lap around the golf course, he saw the toothless old man approaching again. What a character. *Somebody's father from the old country. Barely spoke English. A gentle old coot, out of place in Brentwood, even in the chic blue warmup suit.*

"Probably the poor relation...of an oil sheik!" Burl gasped.

"How are you, fine sir!" the old man cackled.

"Good...good...."

"That is good, fine sir!"

"Yeah—right."

"You are a fine good man, sir!"

Burl puffed past and began a second, wrenching lap. *Have to sweat the weight off.* But deep inside he sensed it was hopeless. He dreaded returning to the clinic on Tuesday for the checkup. He hadn't lost weight. His gut still stuck out unless he held it in. A steak was hard to pass up. Bourbon-and-water with a cigarette was the best way to schmooze clients and survive boring nights on the road.

His last trip had been grueling. Screwed up inventories, missing invoices, slow-paying accounts. Never-ending pressure to solicit new business. Friday night in Kansas City he signed a new client. Lined up two girls so the guy had a choice while leaving Burl one to talk to. It made dinner like a social outing for two couples. But the girls were pros; it was all part of the routine. He'd gotten soused and paid the second girl to spend the night with him.

On the flight home yesterday, a squirming fear had swelled up inside. He stared out the window at ambient clouds. Something was wrong with his life. He studied his trembling hands and vowed repentance. He skipped dinner last night, breakfast this morning. He would restrict himself to fruit juice until the physical. *Any sacrifice to squeeze by, and then reform for good.* He didn't want to go on disability leave or be assigned to the head office. My God--that would drive him nuts. The regional reps--They'd razz holy hell: Big Burl Hardy, packed it in at last!

The long hill was agony when he topped it. Sweat stung his eyes. His running shoes were wet inside, chafing his heel tendons. He headed down slope toward the starting point and decided he could do two more laps. Go out again tomorrow. Once more the toothless old man came into view, his gait jaunty, arms gangly. *Only the poor are thin and enjoy it. Why don't the old fart's relatives have a dentist pull that ugly tooth?* Burl grunted the ritual greeting, unnerved by the cadaverous body sliding past his sweat-blurred vision.

On the third lap the sun blazed. The hill punished every cell in his body. His legs barely carried him. He breathed in rasping gulps to suck air into his parched lungs. Scenery swirled, his mouth bubbled a bitter brew. *Was it so long ago, offensive left guard, first string?* Neither the workouts nor the games wore him down. Exertion had stimulated, brought his body to life, filled him with a manliness that was sated only by drinking and whoring. God…the best of times…he could go on…forever.

Downward leg, third mile of the hot and humid torture. He sensed a flush of strength, as if aglow with vitality. Even the sight of the old man did not disturb him. Then his heart exploded into his throat. The old man appeared to jerk like a puppet with tangled strings, a startling, loose-limbed dance, like a crazed skeleton. Roadway, pine trees--golf greens quivered. Burl froze and glared fixedly at the old man.

"Take good look…old bag…of bones!" he gasped. The world gyrated. "Maybel!" The sky jammed both eyes, boulders smashed into his ears. A corrosive pain struck his chest. He smacked into the pavement. His arms and legs stiffened in a violent convulsion. Urine blasted through his penis as he shrieked. "Ohhh...HELLLLL!"

He couldn't move. There came a face. Brown, thin, wrinkled as dry earth. The eyes black marbles. The mouth opened and closed, its yellow-green snaggle tooth jutting below the upper lip like antique aged ivory.

"Are you perfectly fine, good sir?" the old man asked, his voice far away.

"Whaaa!" Burl's mouth pebbled with fragments of his broken partial plate. "Whaa!" He expelled denture fragments onto the asphalt.

"You must make yourself fine, sir!" the old man said.

Burl wanted to push the sonofabitch away, but he couldn't. His body quaked free of his willpower. *Toothless old man! Get away...from me!* Burl stared, viewing his own red face with swollen cheeks, missing teeth, and graying hair. With a massive, terminal convulsion, gravity pressed him into the roadway. He had arrived on the scene to attend himself. *Who'd get new clients? Take care of poor Maybel? Block off tackle...on a fullback dive?* Who would...his heart quaked, waned, dimming eyes locked on the gaunt, brown specter hovering above him. Intense blue morning sky broiled with sunshine--and life.

How could such a craggy old man, wiry and cruddy with wrinkles, seem so full of vitality when he--Burl Hardy--had to convulse in hapless despair on the ground, muscles spasming as the sun liquified? Why was it so...so inevitable? He sensed himself losing weight finally, shedding pounds as if sliced from his bones in great slabs of prime masculinity. It only needed discipline, willpower to...to....

The toothless old man hesitated over the motionless hulk, bony hands on his knees, then straightened himself, sighed an Old World exhalation of humble acceptance, and ambled across the golf course with his jerk-jointed gait seeking aid for a fallen pilgrim. Needle-rustling pines stirred and shimmered with a refreshing breeze as life eased onward.

CLEO'S SERPENT

On the Saturday afternoon that would be his last of indolent, elderly freedom, Otis Pembroke sat watching boys play baseball in the park. It was a hot, dry day that petrified the lungs with each breath. The wood bench pressed against his aged thighs through the denim pants as if to smooth seven decades' flesh. It was not a discomfort that he minded. Better than lounging uselessly in the residence his son and daughter-in-law intended for him. It was pleasant observing the ball game, remembering vivid sandlot days.

A shout of athletic excitement erupted from the park playing field; that was followed by raucous cheers from moms and dads. Otis had placed himself alongside the left foul line of the outfield. As he watched the Little League game he recognized a few players. He'd seen so many games over years that they melded into one boy--freckled, spunky. He viewed them in his mind listening at the window of his apartment a block away.

It was a suburban park, but nestled against a fenced cattle range. Family houses nudged open acreage. Hence the signs near the grassy outfield: *Danger! Rattlesnakes are a natural part of this field. Please be alert and cautious.* The warning was also in Spanish with *Peligroso!* and a realistic picture of a coiled rattlesnake. As often as Otis had been in the park, including the weed patch beyond the baseball field, he'd never once encountered a snake. Gophers, squirrels, rabbits and lizards--but caretakers kept the field safe for the athletic children.

What he most enjoyed about the rustic scene wasn't just the shade from tall eucalyptus trees, but the chance to drift through memory tunnels. A lanky boy running the bases amid yells echoed in his reverie. He heard his name from a farmhouse porch: *O-TEEES!* He revisited the smell of sun-baked grass bordering wheat fields and sage mingling with mustard seed and wild oak. Yes, what he liked about sitting in the shade was that it made him feel a vital participant in the parade of existence. His long life came back to him more vividly in the outdoors than in the quiet of his apartment.

He recalled his father, touching a match to kerosine-doused dried branches and shrubs piled high for months ready for burning. And the snakes. They'd nestled in the security of the brush over hot afternoons. As they tried to flee, his father scooped them up with a rake to be tossed onto the blazing pyre. Small and large alike writhed and roasted in sizzling agony, adding a seared meaty stench to his childhood recollection. There was something about snakes; cobras in a pit as he squirmed watching an early movie version of *The Jungle Book*. What was it about snakes? Coiled, hissing, striking, slithering, threatening pain, disability--eternal slumber.

He could never get over Cleopatra and the asp. How many times had he seen the scene? Claudette Colbert pressing fangs to her breast in the 1930s? Elizabeth Taylor and the basket of figs in the 1960s? An ivory hand in harm's way, a sting--followed by the numbing progress of oblivion. Otis had never been bitten, but he could imagine it from bumblebee stings one day when he'd led a horse in from the field. Bees the size of pecans had smacked the horse's sweat-lathered neck and drooling muzzle, two or three bouncing into Otis's face like bullets; his flesh swelled for a week, and he was so sick he couldn't keep food down.

He stiffened on the bench, clutching the ebony cane in his moist palms. For no reason, he felt uneasy. It must be regret, the idea that he'd never again be so free, able to just be himself. He stood slowly, waited out the momentary dizziness as his heart rate adapted to standing, watched the game for a few more moments, and then walked around the edge of the field. He stayed on the dirt path amid the grass and weeds. Having trod this dusty way often and never once seeing anything notable, it wasn't surprising that the indolent snake at first failed to register in his sight. It might have been a tree branch, so still in the mottled eucalyptus leaves and grass. If an illusion, it was a *real* illusion.

But there it lay, serpentine, deadly in its beauty, arrow-shaped head close to the ground, its russet length soaking sun in naked, glossy pleasure. Otis stood mute in paralyzed fascination. As many times as he had encountered rattlesnakes in his lifetime, they never failed to stun him into total immobility. It was primal, built into the reptilian knob atop his spinal cord. He couldn't suppress a hundred thousand years of his species' fear of the satanic nemesis or primate ancestry preceding *homo sapiens* by eons. A shout from the baseball infield assailed his ears, but he gazed only at the rattlesnake that eyed him while flicking its tongue.

At first Otis had a petty thought, but it persisted as he shifted his weight to lean more on his cane. Images of the old folks' residence flitted across his mind almost in synch with the flickering tongue now probing ahead as the snake, sensing a presence beyond the sun's warmth, slithered toward

HUNCHING HOMEWARD

the grass of the baseball outfield. Otis didn't will it, but nonetheless he ambled ahead as well. It would be easy to tote the snake into the open field with his cane, but he courted danger by placing himself ahead of its agitated progress. His shoes offered no protection, nor the soft fabric of his denim pants. It didn't matter. His mouth became prairie grass dry as he started to fantasize the impact of fangs. If Cleopatra had courage to do it, why couldn't he? What was so grand about wasting away in bed when peace from a natural syringe awaited nearby?

He quickened his pace to head off the snake's escape, oblivious to the crescendo of yells from the baseball field. Confronting the snake in its flight, Otis was thrilled to see it rear back, not coiling, but alarmed, not rattling, but twitching. At that fierce moment he didn't know how to go about getting bitten. He couldn't emulate Cleopatra and place his hand close. The only way was to let the thing bite him on the leg. Thunder in his ears. Shouts, screams, the ground nearby vibrating through the soles of his shoes.

Running steps, feet pounding hard alkali earth. He approached the snake even as he glanced over his shoulder to see a baseball-capped boy running toward him in pursuit of a bouncing ball coming toward Otis. He squawked a warning at the wide-eyed boy just as the baseball smacked his left leg at the same instant his right calf received a piercing sting. Both knocked him breathless, as did a bite in the flesh above the ankle. He reeled back, his eyes engulfed by endless sky as a gorge rose in his belly.

Surreal images: Otis swinging his cane at the boy to keep him away; beating the coiled rattlesnake till it quivered in death; himself hobbling on his left leg while the right throbbed with terrifying numbness; boys crowding about as Otis sank to the grass. After unending noise and confusion, adults and boys gathered around him. A coach-like man used his whistle cord to tourniquet Otis's lower leg. Minutes later he heard a siren like the wail of a wounded animal. Paramedics placed a crystalline oxygen mask over his nose and mouth. Sunlight patches amid swaying eucalyptus branches. Cleopatra reclining in blissful demise as he was wheeled to an ambulance. Vertigo during the throbbing ride as fog engulfed him.

When he awoke it wasn't to a domain of ethereal whiteness and heavenly peace, but an emergency room smelling of astringent and asepsis. It was not a new experience. His stroke five years before, hip surgery--he'd had his share of medical encounters. But this was unique because he was with total strangers: a baseball coach and three women. He was comforted and praised beyond simple concern. It appeared, as he listened during treatment involving needles and an anti-venom shot, that he'd done something heroic; saved the boy fielder from certain snakebite.

When his son and daughter-in-law arrived an hour or so later and were also regaled with Otis's act of bravery, he was tempted to confess what he had foolishly been about. But the fuss magnified, and his son stroked matted gray hair Otis kept GI short. Grateful parents considered him more than just another oldster sitting on a bench. During the week in the hospital, boys and parents visited. A reporter from the newspaper gave Otis an opportunity to explain that he'd only done what anybody would have. They printed his picture. He was adopted by the Little Leaguers for the summer and sat in the bleachers. No old folks home just yet; he remained in the game, at least for one more season.

AN OLD MIRROR

Maple frame dried and grainy, silver flaking around the edges. Wendell noticed the derelict mirror in an antique and collectibles shop across the Mississippi in Alton, Illinois. It was an indolent, spring Saturday in late April, and he'd loitered through five dusty shops seeking nothing more than to slay hours before returning to his apartment by Forest Park in St. Louis. Most of the stores reeked of mildew and mite flecks, even though owners tried to maintain cleanliness. Old furniture, clothing, dishes, and pots and pans defied orderliness; they also conveyed an irretrievable sense of a time lost never to return. Not even Wendell's nostalgia could restore newness to artifacts left by anonymous owners. He sneezed into his kerchief.

He was tempted, gazing obliquely at the mirror, to apply his handkerchief to wipe the dust-crusted surface. Angled against the brick wall on top of an oak dresser about the same vintage, it looked turn-of-the-century. That would make it maybe seventy-five years old. Who could say for sure? If so, it was at least a quarter century old when he was born in

1925. And now he was fifty--only half the longevity required to officially be an antique himself. With care he wiped his handkerchief over the glass, exposing streaks of yellowed silver patina much like old brass. Expecting nothing more than a sharper reflection, he was startled to view instead the sober eyes of a rakish young man who stared at him, brushy black walrus moustache, fusty full eyebrows, hair parted slickly in the middle.

The sudden appearance rocked him backward enough to bump the crusted iron frame of a bedstead. It creaked under his assault as he steadied himself with one hand. He was embarrassed and tried to control his rapid breathing. He gazed, thinking he'd made a mistake. Perhaps it was not a mirror after all, but the highly glazed surface of a photographic portrait---oval and upright. He approached slowly, handkerchief poised to remove more surface grime. As he did so, the image appeared to slither sideways into the beveled edges and fade away. His own presence suffused the silvered plane. The image that had so startled him was gone. He gazed, straight on, then at an angle, and tried to view what had shocked him, but viewed only himself---gaunt, flat gray hair on his smooth pate, watery blue eyes trying to see what had startled him.

He proceeded to wipe the surface as clean as possible, smearing grime where his now encrusted handkerchief could no longer produce a shine. Glancing behind he noted the shop owner staring over the top of her granny glasses with tight brown eyes. She said nothing, but a jowly grimace suggested that he'd better not be up to no good and was being tolerated only as a potential customer. Innocently, he peeked at the mirror and beheld a new reflection; not antique junk, but another figure looking outward as if at an amber-glassed window. It was a woman in a high-button dress and lace collar, auburn tresses burnished by the sepia tone photograph.

When he faced the mirror full on, the image faded, fog-like, leaving only his own perplexed visage.

His eyes watered, and he almost wiped them with the handkerchief until he realized filth from the grimy mirror would do more harm than good. A deft touch of his shirtsleeve across both eyes helped. By then, what he saw in the mirror was merely himself, fragile, looking older than his half century, with a pitiful aspect that made him feel pathetic that he had to seek novelty in imaginary companions. The single mirror in his apartment was on the medicine cabinet door that he gazed into when shaving his prickly gray whiskers each morning. That was his ritual to avoid looking at himself, focusing instead on lean strokes with the safety razor, and afterward, the path of the stiff-bristled brush flaying strands of thinning hair against his freckled scalp. Gazing into the ancient mirror, he realized that he hadn't really studied his face in years. What was the point? Why bother with a depressing examination of inevitable aging?

He turned away from the mirror and continued his errant amble through the shop, but kept glancing back at it surreptitiously as though he half expected another person to gaze at him. What he observed each time was a kaleidoscopic reflection depending on his viewpoint: bright sky through the shop window bouncing off the mirror, a crazy-quilt pattern comprised of an iron bed post and assembled furniture. He saw no more figures, man or woman, from the past, staring into his trivial present.

It came to him that he spent mindless hours in such stores because they organized time in a manner he found satisfying. How did time smell? Like dried leaves. How did it sound? Soft as wind past a drape. How did it feel? Like static electricity prickling bare skin. It was a comforting contemplation despite the crypt-like atmosphere of most antique and curio shops. But as much as he tried to interest himself in other oddities, his mind drifted back to the mirror, obsessing on the images, lingering over an amazement that still made him shiver in spite of the torpid heat surging from grated floor level ducts. He headed to the front door, ready to leave. Then an itchy impulse urged him to ask the shopkeeper about the mirror--its age, price, and origin.

She didn't know how old it was or where it'd come from--a local house or farm possibly. She had it priced at seventy-five dollars, but would consider sixty. He abruptly offered fifty, settled for fifty-five, and before he sensed that he had done something rash and foolish, was carrying it toward his Pontiac sedan. He placed it face up in the trunk, deciding it was only a mirror and not some magical artifact. Reassured, as well as subdued, he saw trunk lid and sky reflected and confined the mirror to darkness as he drove to his apartment. He had no notion where he'd hang it; maybe in his bedroom next to the maple dresser. He tried to suppress the unsettling emotion it had induced, an eerie intuition that he'd come upon something out of the ordinary, magical, possibly supernatural.

He lugged it into the apartment and placed it turned to the wall on the floor beside the dresser. Time to think about it later, after he decided whether he wanted it anywhere in his life. The more he thought about what he'd done, how stupid the purchase, the more disconsolate he felt, not only with his foolishness, but his empty existence. The notion that it was more than a grimed mirror, that he'd merely been intrigued by mysterious figures in its depths, unnerved his sensible self-image. Was such a purchase the beginning of frivolous behavior that accompanied aging? Senility? Dementia? He hoped not, but couldn't dismiss the morbid notion.

Two weeks later he noticed it against the wall. In the busyness of his work as a payroll bookkeeper he had forgotten about it. Also, his sleep had been restless, filled with weird dreams where he was younger but as indecisive and inconspicuous as he knew he was---and from which he partially awakened disoriented and miserable because he lacked the resolve to be other than what he was. He turned the mirror outward but left it on the floor as he gazed at the image of his slippered feet and the vastness behind them under the bed. Nothing else was reflected now. He forgot about it until later that night, lying in bed, when he looked downward and, indistinct at first, then with heart-stopping clarity, saw two children: a boy in Little Lord Fauntleroy suit and a blonde-curled girl with lace and ribbons. Both smiled at him in time's peeling reflectance. He blinked and stared till they gently floated away into the indistinct beveled edges.

Saturday morning, he got hammer and nails, placed the mirror over the maple dresser, stood back to measure the effect, and acknowledged that, junky as it was, it gave the room a timeless quality. Furthermore, gazing at himself, he liked what he saw; not that he'd changed, but at least he looked *significant*. It wasn't much, but better than he appeared in his bathroom cabinet mirror. But the best part, after a few days and having wiped the glass with soft towels, was that he saw the young man again; also the woman; and the children.

He sensed that, mystical or not, the mirror somehow had acquired the capacity to retain, and reflect some hearty souls who had gazed into it at one time or another. These people didn't acknowledge him, but it was enough that they simply appeared now and then, There were no family memories he could dredge up to palliate his sad nature; no beloved photos of parents or grandparents, nor siblings. He lived a solitary existence, and treasured the ghostly images. Also, he too might one day participate in that mirror dominion and re-exist on some other's bedroom wall. Surely a fantasy, but it brought a pittance of soulful contentment.

RICHARD VAUGHN

Over the expanse of months and years, the mirror became the most important aspect of his leisure, surpassing television, visiting shops, and simply enduring. He not only met many other long dead companions, courtesy of the mirror's capacity for bringing past lives forward, but was also gratified to see that when he posed before it, his own form lingered when he turned away, an after-image much like that when the eyes quickly close leaving the world on the optic nerve as though reluctant to fade. That, as much as his joy in being part of its mysterious nature, made it his most treasured possession. The great hope grew that, when his earthly span was over, he would become an actor in that silvered world, and a visual presence viewed by a future needy soul--perhaps another temporarily mortal ghost very much like himself.

WEEP NO MORE

Herman paused at the outer door to his office. It hadn't been a good day and would only get worse. He felt weak and empty. His heart beat only enough to sustain life without making it worthwhile. His tie was loosened, and he carried his black suit coat draped over one arm. He wiped his puffy face on his shirtsleeve. The BETSAL WHOLESALE NOVELTIES letters gracing the frosted door panel seemed devoid of significance. He shoved the door open.

"Don't get up, Buddy," he said to the lean young man who had never gotten over the habit of rising whenever somebody entered. "It's terminally hot outside."

He chuckled as he always did at his witticisms before realizing that it was not amusing, especially today.

"How was the funeral, Mr. Betz?" Buddy asked, his face a mask of perpetual sympathy.

"Fantastic. Really fantastic in every way."

Herman tossed his coat over the oak swivel chair. His desk took all the space in front of the wide front window where he could watch the traffic along Wilshire Boulevard.

He searched several drawers before finding a cigar. It took three matches to get it going because he couldn't seem to catch enough breath. Then he glanced at the sales orders piled on the desk, avoiding the empty desk nearby.

"Mr. Muhlson called," Buddy said. "It was about--"

"Those goddamn Chink watches. What's his number?"

While Buddy flipped through the desktop card file, Herman rested his head in the palms of his hands, letting the fingers caress the throbbing temples and press the gray-brown hair to the back of his damp neck. Buddy knocked the index box onto the floor. As cards slithered over the vinyl, Buddy stood holding one he'd removed.

"You're gonna go a *long* way." Herman said. Sal had kept track of everything before she got sick. Her desk now showed only a beige phone and *Portagee* red wine ceramic vase holding a dusty assortment of plastic daisies. A cumulus of blue-green smoke curled from the oval of his mouth toward the cottage cheese plaster ceiling. "A long way."

"Muhlson's number is 531-1012."

"I bet Sheffler is hot for them watches, too." Herman poked the buttons like a man trying to puncture the shell of the phone receiver. "The greedy bastard."

He placed the cigar on the edge of the desk and closed his burning eyes as he listened to the irritant buzz on the line. He slammed the phone down. Buddy had retrieved the index cards and began sorting them back into the metal box.

"Busier'n hell. Sheffler's sure as hell after those watches." Herman picked up his cigar and pulled on it long and hard for a blast of smoke that stung his tongue. "On this one order I could clear enough to pay for Sal's funeral."

"More condolences came about Mrs. Betz," Buddy said.

"Dump 'em. She's dead now. I don't want her old cronies' driveling about what a swell person she was. There were so many I didn't know at the funeral I felt like a goddamned visitor. Out of more'n fifty people I only knew maybe half a dozen."

Buddy sat down at his desk. For a while he shuffled papers. He dropped the unopened sympathy cards into a green plastic wastebasket like dew-laden leaves.

"Remind me to get funeral insurance," Herman said. He cleared his throat and wiped his eyes. "On second thought, screw it. Let someone else pay. Goddamn mortuaries bleed the living to bury the dead."

He listened to his labored breathing, totally mortal. Rays of sunlight rippled through the half-closed, ivory-colored wood blinds as he waited. The phone rang. He grabbed it quick.

"That you, Sheffler?" He settled in his chair. "Yeah, too bad. Didn't know she was sick until I got back from Phoenix. All happened so fast--yeah, she was a great gal." He cleared his throat and clutched the cigar tighter. "Watches? Hell, I don't know. Muhlson didn't say. Even if he had, I wouldn't cadge them from you."

He put the cigar on the edge of his desk at the spot marked by the burn in the formica. It rolled onto the floor as if flicked. He realized his shaking hand had done it. He reached down as the cigar slipped under the desk. Buddy came over to pick it up. Herman motioned to snuff it in the ashtray, where it smoldered in the ember stench of dying ash.

"Sheffler, old buddy. This is Herm, remember? Give Muhlson an upside offer and you've got them. Five thousand? Way too much. Leave room for a markup. I'd have to go five. You, not that much. Try four thou. Yeah, okay--later."

Buddy stood with his hands in his denim pockets after Herman had hung up, and finally said, "I thought you wanted those watches."

"I do, but that sonofabitch Sheffler is playing me."

Herman punched a number and ran his free hand through his gray hair.

"Muhlson? Yeah, Betz. About those Chink watches... yeah, nice funeral. Well attended. Look, I was hoping to bid--oh? Forty-five hundred? Too bad, because I'd go five thou. Don't want to screw the other offer. Okay, if that's all right with you. I'll send a check."

He leaned back in his chair, momentarily buoyant despite his fatigue.

Buddy came to him. "Here are the rayon T-shirt invoices."

"Helluva world," Herman said, his gaze on the door sign. "When you're on top, like Muhlson, guys like me hafta jump. Nothing to do but take it."

"I guess so, sir."

Herman grabbed the phone on the first ring.

"Yeah, Sheffler--five thousand? Who bid it up? Well, you can't get them all. They're not worth it. Yeah, okay, lunch tomorrow at the deli."

He put the phone down, his brow wrinkled as he waited.

Finally Buddy asked, "Should I take a check to Muhlson?"

"Not yet. Sheffler's gonna jerk the price up, sure as hell." When the phone didn't ring, he began pacing. Every wall was bare except near the door where the business licenses hung in thin, glassless black frames. "Me'n Sal, thirty years. Couldn't afford a place to stay. Had a mattress in here. What a time that was."

"Mrs. Betz used to talk about it when you were out."

Herman tried to clear his throat. The room felt stuffy. When he raised the blinds a film of dust made him sneeze several times. He pushed the window open six inches and stared out at the surging, restless traffic.

HUNCHING HOMEWARD

"She was just Sal," he said. "Get drunk, mess around--she was a swell sport. Not much to look at, but one helluva hard worker...."

He turned to see Buddy looking at him. He wiped his face on his damp shirtsleeve. The phone rang. He let it ring seven times before answering.

"Yeah--Muhlson. Fifty-five hundred? Steep." He sat in his chair, opened the desk drawer, studied his checkbook. "Maybe fifty-eight tops. Yeah, okay, thanks."

He tossed the phone toward the receiver. It missed, bounced on the desk and fell to the floor. Buddy put it back as Herman hit the desk top with his clenched fist.

"Sheffler! That lousy sonofabitch! He knew I needed them. He's bid up the price. That's payback for those Mexican neckties last year."

He raged and paced the room until the phone rang again.

"Sheffler? Fifty-eight hundred, fer crissakes! Hell, no, I won't let you buy lunch. What's the idea? Aw, hell...yeah...okay...noon tomorrow. Right, even up."

He put the phone down. His eyes swelled with tears. Herman pulled out his handkerchief, wiped at his face but only brushed past his eyes.

"One goddamned cruddy joke. Whole damned life. One cruddy joke with a crappy punch line." He wiped his eyes again, then glared at the embarrassed boy. "What the hell you waiting for? Messenger the fifty-eight hundred to Muhlson."

"You've got the checkbook, Mr. Betz."

"Oh, hell, sure--sorry, kid."

Herman wrote the check so fast the amount no longer meant anything. He handed it to Buddy, who phoned a messenger service, placed it in the pouch, and started downstairs to the pickup box.

"Go home," Herman said with great weariness "Have some fun."

"Thank you, sir. See you in the morning."

"Another day," Herman said after Buddy closed the door.

There were no more cigars. Traffic on Wilshire Boulevard roared past the open window. After a while he stopped pacing, glanced unavoidably at her old desk, then sat at his. Lamentable minutes later, as the orange sun slipped behind the eucalyptus tree line, he put his head down on his arms and grieved for his departed wife, and the other life she had taken away with her.

TURN ABOUT

Haskell barely recognized his son. The man who entered the restaurant waited to be seated by the hostess. It'd been almost twenty years. What was he now--forty-eight? He was husky in a light gray sport coat and charcoal slacks; Haskell scrutinized him trying to fathom himself or his wife in the ruddy complexion, wide face, and blue-gray eyes. His breath fluctuated as he adjusted his silver-framed glasses. Before Haskell realized *he* had been recognized, the man was led to his table by the seating host. He stood, knocking his cane from the arm of the chair; it crashed to the tile floor like a calamity.

"Brendan," he mumbled, wondering if he should attempt to shake hands as he leaned on the table supported by his left arm locked straight down. As it turned out he didn't have to offer. His son gazed as if Haskell had the importance of a parking valet before he seated himself. The hostess gave Brendan a menu, noted Haskell's cane on the floor, retrieved it, presented it to him with a cordial smile, and left.

"Ah, yes, well," Haskell said, sitting back down and making sure the cane was secured against the armrest. "Glad you came."

Haskell's hands trembled with more anxiety than age and arthritis, but he tried to control them as he clutched his menu. Beyond Brendan's left shoulder two empty tables away he noticed the woman, her straight back cloaked in a pale green jacket with sublime curled strands of silver hair touching the collar. How had he missed noticing her on the way to his table, or she missed him? Helene--studying a pamphlet while picking at her salad. He'd forgotten that she sometimes had dinner here but was shocked to see her at lunch. A bad time for an estranged audience as he confronted their son, but no sense fretting about it now.

"Anything look good to you?" Haskell asked Brendan.

"Just what the hell did you invite me here for?"

"Lunch, and maybe catch up with your life."

"*What*," Brendan said, "do you *want*?"

"Alright, have it your way." Haskell put the menu down. "Let's just say that I wanted to see how you turned out."

"Surprised I'm not dead, or wandering about a homeless addict?"

"Not at all. I hoped you'd dig deep and survive somehow."

"Well, I did, without any goddamn thanks to you."

"Untrue, son. Quite a lot of thanks to me."

"Still your sink-or-swim bullshit!"

"Seems to have worked, because here you are."

"Not for long," Brendan said, pushing his chair back.

"Please, tell me about yourself. I put twenty years into you."

"Before you finally threw me to the damned wolves, you mean."

Haskell sensed a shift in Helene's posture behind Brendan, a slight stiffening as if more vigilant, perhaps considering a look about to satisfy suddenly aroused curiosity. The shoulders rose and fell, suggesting full breaths. She'd stopped eating. He wanted to lunge at the boy who'd turned middle-aged, the golden son who carried Haskell's DNA into the future. Instead, he tried to steady himself, fingers intertwined as he soothed gnarled flesh by gentle massage.

"Wolves--an apt canine metaphor," he said as serenely as he could. "When I was your age, it would have been called 'going to the dogs.'"

"How quaint. It was more like a lousy bastard and my traitorous Mom."

"Memory rationalization. You dropped out of college a third time after two drug rehabs, wanting money for another cross-country trip with your reefer buddies."

"I simply needed to get away from a really bad scene."

"Your plan was to keep acting it out on the road."

"That was your bullshit way of looking at it."

"We went broke trying to get you straight. The cash you wanted was for your sister's education. You blew it, so I stopped the financial bleeding."

"And how is dear, sweet Belinda?"

"Doing okay. She suggested this lunch."

"She would. So, she was a good investment?"

"College, financial advisor, married, two boys in high school."

"You must be thrilled. Dumping me worked great, right? You got the grandkids you wanted. The clan marches on. Seems everybody's happy."

"No parent's ever pleased about losing a child," Haskell said, noting the now fully alert posture Helene displayed without turning. "But life's one lousy crapshoot. The way genes are scrambled, who knows what nature will put in each kid? We gave you the best chance we could. When you turned self-destructive, we placed our bet on Belinda."

"How cold-blooded, professional. Cut your damned losses and moved on?"

"You see it as Darwinian. Survival-of-the-fittest. But-- I'd do it again."

"That's not exactly news. How did you manage to find me?"

"Not hard when even people who hide can be found."

"So what's this about? Let's kiss and make up?"

"Don't expect that. It's mostly about lunch."

"You must be kidding! So unbelievable."

"That's actually why I invited you."

"It's so out of character you'd do this."

"You look well, Brendan. Straight now?"

"Sure as hell am, not that it matters to you."

"You've grown up. Let me admire your success."

Brendan shook his head. "This isn't happening."

"I understand you're married. Have children?"

"Two daughters. Does Mom know about this?"

"I didn't tell her, but...she found us out."

"How the hell did she do that?"

"Fate. She's behind you."

Brendan looked back as Helene turned to see her son and Haskell. He didn't hear what she said but her lips formed, 'I've missed you' for one, or both, of them.

"Dammit!" Brendan said. "What kind of bullshit setup is this?"

Haskell shrugged. "I honestly didn't know she'd be here."

Brendan got up. "What the hell do you *people* want?"

"Nothing at all," Helene said, scrutinizing Haskell.

Brendan left, pushing out the restaurant door.

A waiter hovered, having kept his distance, for which Haskell was grateful. His ex-wife turned away. He read the menu for a while before limping over beside her. She didn't look at him as she sipped coffee, cradling the cup as if a magic potion. He loved her hands, thin and adroit, the way her touching simple objects became special. It was a gift that enabled her to artfully embrace reality while he labored to possess it.

    He sighed. "I just wanted to see him after all these years."

    "Yes, I know," she said, gazing at him. "Please…sit."

    "Thanks. Well, as a witness, what do you think?"

    "Stubborn, Hask. Like you. An inherited trait."

    "He's half you as well," Haskell said, unable to forget that she wanted room to be herself seven years ago. "You look quite well, contented, the person you aspired to be."

    "In a way I suppose I am," she said without any trace of pride.

    "What do you do with all that freedom you longed for?"

    "Doesn't Belinda keep you informed? I thought she was the liaison since we've gone our separate ways. You know, Daddy's little girl?"

    "I've made a pact with her," Haskell said. "No gossip about you, or me. Has she kept her word, or are you up on my mundane existence?"

    "As good as her word, merely confirming that you're doing okay." She pressed the coffee cup to her lips, but didn't drink. "Have we lost Brendan…forever?"

    He realized that she'd said *we* when she could as easily have said *I*. Brendan had been *hers*, and Belinda *his*, although such crude parental ownership was an invitation for strife. In fact, Brendan had been the indulged child, for which he blamed himself despite Helene's rapt smothering. Haskell hadn't been able to spoil Belinda because she had a tough sensibility that neither he nor Helene could corrupt. It was that natural selection mystery that produced a trait not easily noted in either parent.

    "Nothing's forever," he sighed, "except perhaps biological anomaly."

"He's still very bitter, and feels betrayed," she said. "By both of us."

"Reveling in the game of 'turnabout is fair play' for cruel emphasis."

"Maybe Belinda could," she said, "might…no. They're not close…yet."

"Brendan's a father now, with hard choices ahead. Maybe he'll get wise."

"That's it, we await wisdom? Before we're abandoned on an ice flow?"

"It's the law of life," he said. "By the way, why're you here at lunchtime?"

"Belinda set it up, then phoned me here and cancelled at the last minute."

"Ah." *Belinda.* He signaled for the waiter. "Can you stay, Helene?"

"Of course. I don't think *we're* into turnabout…or, are we?"

Haskell relaxed. Lunch might be salvaged after all.

RESPIRATION

Sense told Beal it was daytime, but his perspective revealed dirty gray fog that reminded him of night. The visibility fluttering between the blinds could also be from moonbeams or lights on the tree-lined street outside his convalescent home window. That was on his left, wire-latticed glass; to his right, waving in the breeze of the ceiling air conditioning vent, hung polyester folds of a white curtain held aloft by hooks to an aluminum track draping it around the metal bed like a funereal shroud. He wanted to ask where he was, what he was doing here, and--who was he?

He wasn't punctured with needles or tubed as he'd been previously, but that didn't mean he wouldn't be tortured in some unique way at any second. He was, however, despite clarity of mind, narcotized to the point of having no physical sense of his body. It didn't matter so long as he could ruminate when he felt a need to escape. He didn't mind being pampered, but there was only a modest amount of sufferance he'd stand before his innate need to be left alone emerged. He had reached that plateau of irritation during turbulent hours stretching back in time.

How long had he been here? A couple days, perhaps a week? Longer? No way to recall time's passage. Lying in state while the rest of the world went about its labors had turned him into a somber witness of mankind's palsied busyness. How did he endure such madness during forty-odd years as an electrical engineer? It was insanity to engage in habitual living when the majesty and mystery of human existence itself lay revealed in every breath a man took. He had thought in moments of reflection that when his final time came he'd be tormented with regrets about things left undone, wants postponed until too late, adventures abandoned in the relentless pace of the mundane and the necessary.

When he wearied of this rapturous contemplation, he focused on his rasping respiration--bellows beneath arched ribs inflating and deflating like sheep's bladders--septic air expelled in a flush. While he did his utmost to breathe deep, sustain a rhythm instead of relying on the body's biologic program, he couldn't monitor himself for more than two minutes before exhaustion set in and he was forced to give in to the life-force that had pulsated for over eight decades. Great God! Finite days and nights played out in an ocean of infinity, one cognitive mammal among billions in an eternity of stars rushing from each other in a cosmic stampede.

He detected a vibration, familiar and strange simultaneously, of someone calling him from a screened back porch as he lounged boyishly in the grass-green yard reeking of summer heat and fluttering moths darting through apple tree-shaded columns of dazzling light. *Leonard Boy! Suppertime!* An elderly voice resonating with authority, compassion and prairie sensibility. How could he respond to such a sinuous invitation pinioned to the bed and dependent on pink-smocked matrons for his every need? It wasn't Grandma, rather a nurse addressing him by his youth name even if his wife, Waylie, had called him Beal. The nurse fluffed his pillow to ease neck and shoulder strain, took his pulse while silently counting with pinched, liverish lips.

She spoke to him in a husky singsong cadence that didn't require that he reply even if he could. That was a side-benefit of his stroke; it wasn't necessary to agree with the inanity of what people said. He need not even fabricate civility, a heartfelt blinking of his watery eyes enough to convince Waylie when she visited that he understood even if he didn't give a damn. They talked for themselves as he had routinely done for most of his semi-conscious life. The nurse emitted a soothing essence, soap probably, or aromatic emollient she'd smoothed over the skin of a man beyond the curtain hacking emphysema so continuously it became natural background noise as if listening to wind gusts through forest cedars, or the cascading sluice of a mountain stream.

The nurse left, quietly, polyester pants slicking sensually across thighs like a well-played cello within a French nocturne. When artificial fibers were viewed in test tubes, did beady-eyed scientists realize they would be adding fresh sound waves to mankind's experience--polyester on polyester--brushed chords in A Flat or B Minor? He imagined he still heard that sublime swish as Nurse continued down the hallway, but of course he couldn't, and he resigned himself once more to measuring his own breaths. *Res-pir-a-tion.* Intake on *res-pir*, outgo on *a-tion*. In some domain of brain tissue, was his electric timer on the verge of catastrophic malfunction? If so, could he be himself until drained of energy and purpose? Was it worth the agony to continue struggling, and to what purpose; life extension? Would he panic if he could no longer inhale-exhale? Was that a life's mandate, trapped in a body with the illusion of freedom?

It was only seconds later that he realized someone else was attending him, a man, thin-faced but with a half smile as though pleased not only with his station in life but the duty he was about to undertake. Before Beal could acknowledge him with a glance, a paper cup was pressed to his lower lip. An esthetically icy thrill followed with a suffusion of pleasure. Oral morphine. It teased the meat-quiver of his tongue to pure delight, suppressing all discomforts visited upon a mortal shell enslaved by debility. It was a release more benign than the needle jabbed into him by a medic near Inchon who strived to relieve the pain from shrapnel that had shredded his leg half a century before. Shit-stench and odor of rotting North Korean bodies assailed his hospice--so much that he felt nauseous. How could he be vomiting a memory?

To respire, he mused, sucking to suppress his gorge. Perchance to dream...was that the rub? Had Shakespeare known opiates? Can we survive, let alone cope, without numbing from without or secreted endogenously? *Reee-spire.* Spiral forever upwards like a cathedral spire, intricate with curlicues, gargoyles and bathetic smiles of saints, or a spiral staircase ascending forever to nowhere, or in ever more heart-beats, to a vaulted cloister in a Gothic novel with the weird and grotesque denizen about to lunge at the heroine? To in-spire, ex-spire, spiraling...the room vibrated around him as he managed to keep his eyes open for fleeting seconds. His whole life had occurred the blink of an eyelid: childhood, school, army, marriage, children, endurance down-shifting till--retire, rhymes with respire, in sync with ex-pire.

Before the next morphine *aperitif* to destroy sensibility, he was aware of gray-blonde hair in tumbling curls vertical to his sight since he'd turned on his right side and Waylie was gazing at him. Waylie Blaisdell Lundy, a fresh-faced farm girl so many years ago it might have been the Middle Ages of his own life. She had always been pretty in a placidly inquisitive way that made him feel she was thinking of nothing or had deep thoughts that would someday burst forth. Beal had often feared she would realize that he was even more pedestrian than herself, and go off in search of excitement without him.

Who was he, after all? Leonard Frederick Beal, written B-i-e-h-l when great grandfather arrived in Minnesota Territory. Germanic genes mingling in a moist womb with a Scottish lass from clan Lundy. Names are lingual DNA, thrusting lineage onward from prehistory, nameless progenitors who must bear some responsibility for Beal and Waylie existing, if briefly. At the moment, Beal was the one whose departure seemed imminent. While he didn't believe in poetic justice because it carried the harsh taint of affectation, the idea seemed entirely appropriate. She was here because--well, she just was. His life, conjoined with Waylie, was circumstantial.

In this paralytic analysis did it mean anything? What purpose had he served throughout millions of seconds--breathing in and out? The children, a son and daughter, recent links in the biological chain extending infinitely back from Beal and Waylie into chaos. They were all stalwart, self-reliant, had visited him, alone or with Waylie, and he wished them well with his waning beneficence. That must be what it meant--every person born at a particular moment in time linking to the next that is to be. Could that be all there really was to the big mystery?

As Waylie clasped his left hand in both of hers, he was shocked to sense the heat in her flesh. She has a fever, the pulsating tissues seeming to sear his fingers with fire. He tried to pull away as from the flame on a gas burner, but couldn't. Then he *knew*. She was alive with warmth, while he'd become ice, a comet tumbling in space. She squeezed, trying to bond his being with hers, but it was too late. A morphine mist cleansed his palate while he swooned. Re-*spire*. *Ree*-spire. *Reee-spire....Reeeee....*

ABOUT THE AUTHOR

Richard Vaughn was born in Illinois in 1933, lived in various towns and cities in Minnesota and North Dakota before moving to California in 1944, and except for two years away in the military and seven years job-related sojourn in St. Louis, Missouri, has lived there since. After a career in Marketing and Advertising, he retired in 1995. Although he participated in writing workshops in Los Angeles and Hollywood over the years, retirement provided the opportunity to devote time toward fiction. After publishing numerous short stories in magazines around the country, a first novel, *Soldier Boys*, about teenage recruits during the Korean War came out in 2004, and was followed in 2005 by a second novel, *Mesa Beach*, a story of conflicted lovers in a California seaside town during the summer of 1963.

These novels were succeeded by short story collections: *Childhood Country, Rapture Runner, Parlous Passion* and *Soshal Scientz. Hunching Homeward*, this fifth collection, includes stories from his childhood and world travels, as well as observations on the everlasting confusion and controversy people encounter coping with the human condition. Of particular interest here is a fascination with mortality and how individuals attempt to accommodate knowledge of the end approaching each life – an inevitability that leads many to extreme and bizarre decisions. What people manage is not necessarily unique in the long span of human history, but remains deeply personal nonetheless and therefore continually fascinating.

Other stories are forthcoming amid the writer's life among his children, grandchildren, and the emerging great grandchildren – surely a sign of aggressive interest at least in the biological life that contributes to a surrogate form of immortality. He lives in Mission Viejo, California.

CPSIA information can be obtained
at www.ICGtesting.com
Printed in the USA
JSHW020729020623
42587JS00001B/74